Murder on the Twelfth Night

Murder
on the
Twelfth Night

by

Tony Hays

Bell Buckle, Tennessee

Library of Congress Cataloging-in-Publication Data

Hays, Tony.
Murder on the twelfth night/Tony Hays
p. cm.
ISBN 0-916078-01-9
1. Shakespeare, William, 1564-1616—Fiction. 2. Dramatists, English—England—Fiction. I. Title.
PS3558.A877M87 1993
813'.54—dc20 93-17088
CIP

For information write: Iris Press, P.O. Box 486, Bell Buckle, TN 37020

Cover and illustration by Holly Lentz-Hays, Manchester, Tennessee.
Page composition by Cascade, Sewanee, Tennessee.

For

Jo Cockelreas, Bo Grimshaw, Richard Tuerk, and Bill McCarron
who told me to write,

and
especially,

Holly,
who never let me quit.

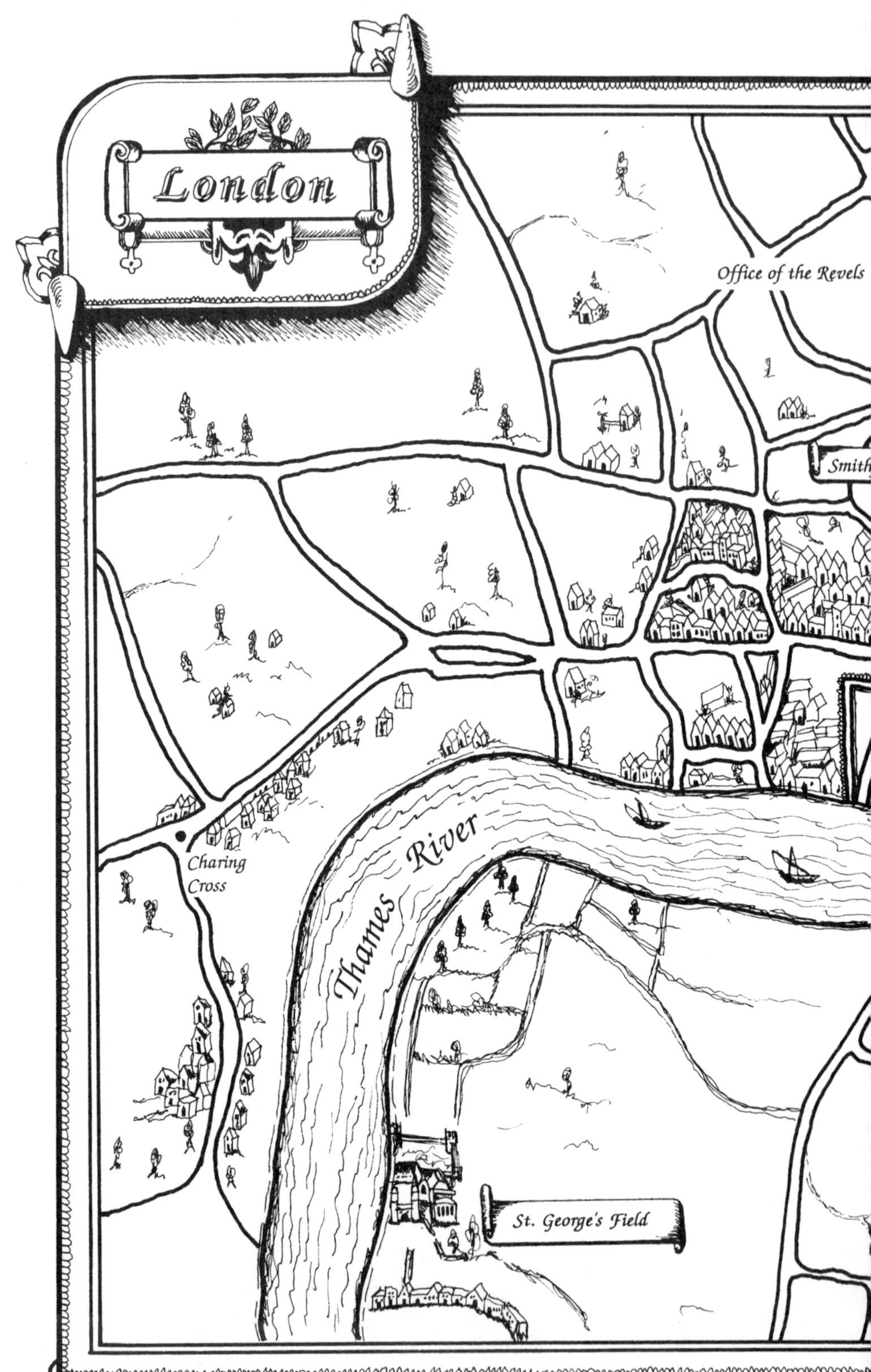
London
Office of the Revels
Smith
Charing Cross
Thames River
St. George's Field

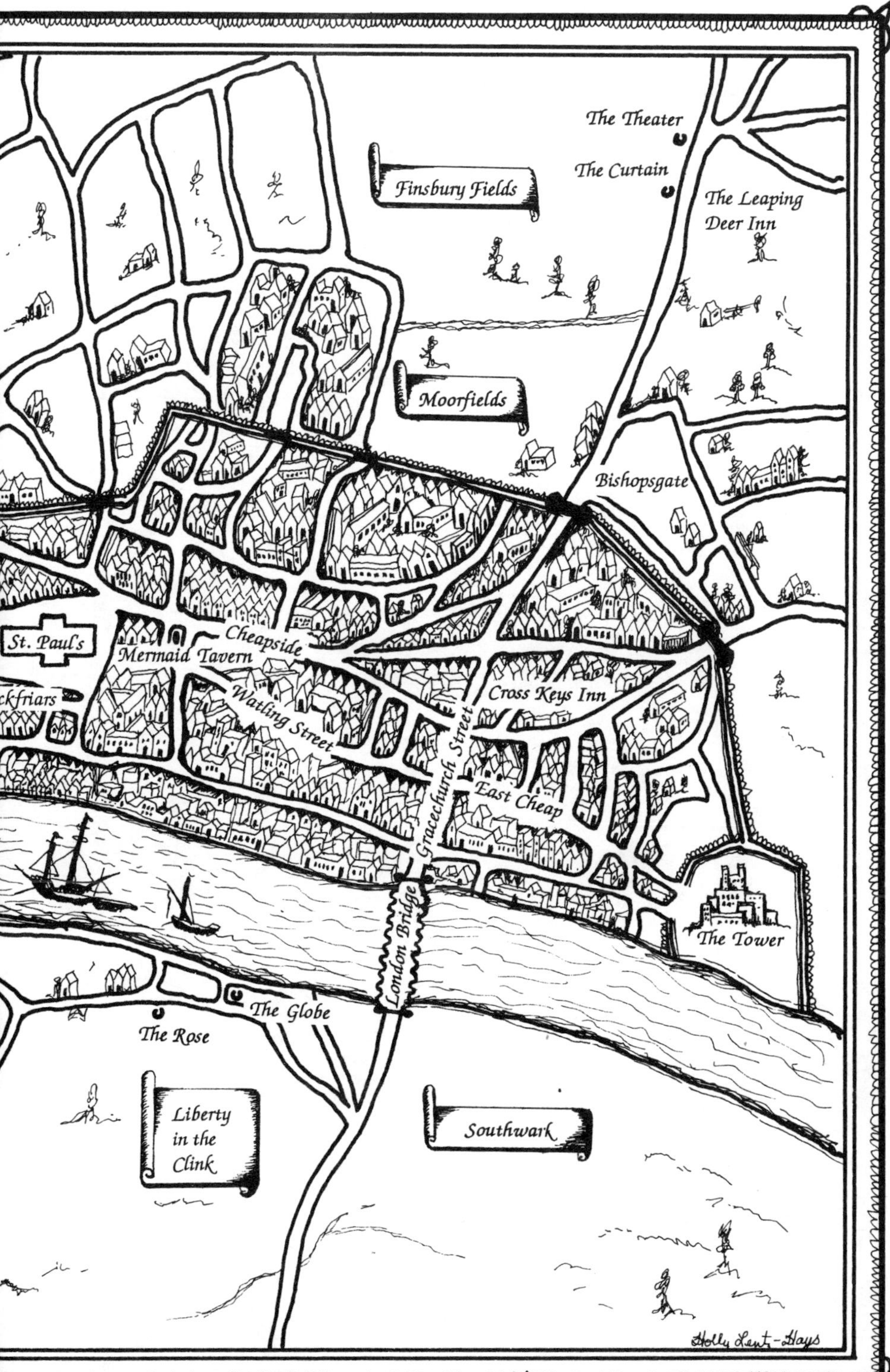
The Theater
The Curtain
Finsbury Fields
The Leaping Deer Inn
Moorfields
Bishopsgate
St. Paul's
Cheapside
Mermaid Tavern
ckfriars
Watling Street
Cross Keys Inn
Gracechurch Street
East Cheap
London Bridge
The Tower
The Globe
The Rose
Liberty in the Clink
Southwark
Holly Lentz-Hays

Dramatis Personae

At the Globe

William Shakespeare, a playwright and actor
Ben Jonson, an apprentice actor
Richard Burbage, an actor
Cuthbert Burbage, the stage manager
Robert Armin, a comedian
Henry Condell, an actor
Allan Hawkins, an apprentice actor and the victim
John Lambert, an apprentice
Arthur Digges, an apprentice
Peter Carew, an apprentice
Harrison of Stratford, a carpenter

In London

Simon Fry, a sailor
Geoffrey Middlebury, a Deputy Sheriff
Clarence Parkes, a constable
Walter Hawkins, a merchant
Ben Jonson, a playwright and bricklayer
John Donne, a lawyer
Susanna Mayo, a girl

Others of Note

Baron Rockford, the Earl of Southampton,
Queen Elizabeth,
and various persons in and around London.

Murder on the Twelfth Night

One

omething wasn't right. Sir Andrew Aguecheek's movements were awkward, mechanical, without his normal skill. His lines flowed well enough, muffled as they were by the kerchief he kept to his nose; but he moved in reaction to the other actors, not with them. And he pressed the duel with Viola too hard; in fact, he pressed his sword in Viola to the hilt.

Shock and pain crossed the face of young Allan Hawkins, who played the role of Viola, and he fell, surprised, to the floor.

A rumble arose from the galleries of the Globe, the wooden benches creaking under their temperamental load, and the groundlings shifted restlessly. In the silence a man shouted, but the words were lost in the three-story, open-roofed building.

Ben Jonson, a young actor idling in the wings and dressed as a serving woman, straightened. He leaned forward as far as he could, yet keeping his head out of the audience's view. "Allan," he hissed. "Allan, you knave! Arise. Tis not in the play. What foolishness is this?" Ben stomped his foot to get Allan's attention. "Allan!"

A hand touched Ben's shoulder and he turned sharply. Richard Burbage, dressed as Duke Orsino, appeared at his elbow.

"Wait, Ben," the older man cautioned. "Something's wrong." Ben followed the actor's eyes and saw the shine of crimson spreading across Allan's costume.

The pair watched as Cuthbert Burbage, Richard's brother and stage-manager at the Globe, strode onto the stage to a chorus of boos and hisses. He knelt beside the crumpled figure and gingerly turned Allan on his back. The bleeding boy offered no resistance.

"Is it part of the play?" a squeaky voice called from the galleries. A dozen voices shouted him down.

"Tis evil!"

"The devil's work!" The cries ran so close together they seemed as one.

Cuthbert, shaggy hair bouncing with each move, looked around, his eyes finally coming to rest on Ben. "Quick, Ben! Go for a surgeon. Some mischief has been performed."

A woman in the crowd shrieked and so did Ben as he spun around to leave and ran into a thin, bearded, and balding man. "Master Shakespeare," the young actor sputtered. "A thousand pardons."

"Perhaps we should rename the play, Ben," William Shakespeare grumbled, straightening his blouse. "It will never see its twelfth night, I'm feared." The younger man flashed a sad smile while the elder dabbed at his own forehead with a kerchief. But Shakespeare stopped the motion in mid-wipe, just as Ben started off again. "Ben," the playwright cried. "Hold! Where is Henry?" Henry Condell, another of the actors, usually capered about in the role of Sir Andrew Aguecheek.

"He was there, Master. Next to Allan, but now . . .," Ben hesitated, searching the growing crowd on the stage for Condell's familiar face. "He's gone." And he was right. The comic figure of Sir Andrew Aguecheek had disappeared.

"On your way, Ben," Shakespeare commanded. "I'll seek out Henry and get to the root of this crippled tree."

Nodding, Ben scooted off the stage and out the main entrance of the Globe, his skirts beating against his legs with each stride and his heart thumping wildly.

Ben had played the role of Maria in every performance of *Twelfth Night,* all eleven, and he was growing tired of the part. Indeed, since he had become a regular member of the company, he was growing tired of playing women's parts at all. With the end of one's apprenticeship usually came other roles, but Ben, though stocky and muscular, was short of stature and fit easily into certain roles, among them those of serving women and the like. But now he pressed on, willing his legs to move faster, for the boy whose blood was spilling on stage, Allan Hawkins, was Ben's best friend.

Allan, two years younger than Ben and still an apprentice, had won the plum job of Viola in *Twelfth Night* and was gaining quite a reputation, Ben knew, on the London stage. Tall and handsome beyond his years, Allan claimed each part he played as his own. His apprenticeship was to end in another year and the owners of the Globe—Shakespeare, Heminges, Burbage, and the rest—would find it difficult to keep him.

Eight years before, William Shakespeare had agreed to take Ben on as his apprentice. It was during those years that Ben met and befriended Allan Hawkins. Players and apprentices led lonely lives and found their closest friends among their colleagues. When Ben's apprenticeship ended the year before, he was honored with an invitation to join the troupe as a regular member and the pair's friendship continued unabated, until that afternoon.

The memory of Allan's blood-stained garments pushed Ben further down the crowded dirt lane, urging him to shove his way through kerchiefed old women moving slowly to market and old men dressed in rags begging for handouts. It was mid-afternoon, but the sun glowed dimly, like a smoky lantern, through the ever present haze in the sky.

"Aaay! Watch your step, lad!" an old man cried. Ben tried to sidestep him and ended up tromping through a stream of sewage on the side of the road. He shook his foot, pushed his way back into the crowd, and kept going.

A surgeon lived not far from the Globe, but it still took several minutes to reach the home of the man, a hunched-over gray-headed codger, in a nearby lane. Ben quickly described his problem.

"Out with you!" the crotchety surgeon stormed, eyeing Ben's

skirt with a cocked brow. "Out! I'll not be part of your perverted activities. Serves you right. Death is all that could come from your heathen ways!"

"Puritan," Ben muttered, stumbling back swiftly to avoid the old man's flailing cane.

Further on, in Southwark and nearer to the entrance to London Bridge, Ben had more luck, finally securing a surgeon more concerned with saving lives than with the perversions of the theater. He latched onto the man and practically dragged him back down the twisting lanes to the Globe.

As they arrived at the elm-framed entrance, the afternoon's audience was streaming from the portal. "Murder!" someone shouted, and Ben picked up his pace, still pulling the surgeon along behind him. Fighting past the crowd, the pair managed to break through and into the theater proper. Ahead, on the stage, Ben saw a mob of people, actors and apprentices mostly, hovering over Allan.

"Out of the way," stormed the surgeon, and the assemblage began scattering. Ben caught a glimpse of his friend as the crowd parted. Allan's doublet and hose were already dyed a deep red and his face had grown pale. Glancing around, Ben saw Richard Burbage sitting alone on the edge of the stage, his head hung so low that his finely pointed beard almost touched his knees. Shakespeare was nowhere to be seen.

"Who here is Jonson?" the surgeon cried.

Ben's head whipped around. "I'm Ben Jonson."

The man's eyes widened. "What, I figured the great Ben Jonson to be a taller tree than this sprout."

A common mistake. Ben was not only short for his twenty years, but nowhere near the stature of his famous namesake. "Aye, I'm Ben Jonson, but not *that* Ben Jonson." Sometimes Ben thought that Shakespeare and Burbage had originally agreed to apprentice him only so they could go through London proclaiming that Ben Jonson was their servant. Shakespeare always enjoyed the chance to irritate his friend, the other Ben Jonson, who was a fellow playwright.

"Come then, young master. This poor lad calls for you. I've done all I can."

Slowly, Ben went to Allan's side and stared down into the pale face. He knelt and took Allan's hand in his.

"Allan, dear friend," he whispered.

"Ben . . .," Allan's voice cracked.

Ben leaned closer. "You must get well, Allan. We have our yearly journey to make. Another season in the country. Just think of the maidens this year, Allan," Ben teased.

"Tweren't Master Henry at the sword, you know." Allan ignored Ben's plea. "I saw it . . . when the scene opened, but had no chance to tell. Don't blame Henry."

"No one will, I promise." Ben nodded.

"I think he looked familiar . . . I cannot be certain . . ." Allan coughed and a thin stream of blood trickled from his mouth. "He kept that damnable kerchief to his face. There is . . . much I would tell you. My father, he must . . ." And then another bloody fit of coughing overtook him. Ben moved away from his friend as the surgeon moved in. A few seconds later the physician looked at Ben and shook his head.

"No!!"

The cry reached above the din of voices and startled Ben. He glanced toward the stage edge and saw a girl with long, brown hair holding her hand to her mouth, a look of pure fright searing across her face. She looked up from Allan's body and her eyes locked with Ben's for just a second. Instantly, she ducked into the crowd, fighting to get away.

"Ben Jonson!" Another voice called the muscular tow-head and he glanced over toward Richard Burbage to see Shakespeare hauling himself out of a trapdoor at centerstage and tossing a tangle of rope on the brown boards.

"What did you discover, Master?" Ben answered without looking, trying instead to follow the mysterious girl, but she had succeeded in getting away.

The playwright planted himself on the edge of the trapdoor with a deep grunt and frowned at Ben. "A bound and gagged Henry Condell. Aye, bound with this very rope." He hefted the strand he had brought through the trapdoor.

Ben took the rope from his former master and studied it—just two pieces of simple hemp, the kind found all about the Globe, linked together in a square knot.

"I loosened him and sent him up to the tiring house to rest," Shakespeare continued. "At any other time I could have enjoyed the sight of Henry gagged, indeed reveled in it— Henry's such a busybody—but with poor Allan in such a shape there is no time for revelry. How is our friend?"

"Gone to Elysium, Master." Though almost a year had passed since Ben's indenture ended, he couldn't bring himself to call Shakespeare "Will." Old habits were indeed hard to break.

"Truly?"

"Truly. His last words were of his father."

"Poor lad," Shakespeare exclaimed. "To come to such an end."

"And the devil's time we'll have now," added Richard Burbage, twisting around. "We have enough trouble keeping our doors open with half of London protesting our plays. Now the London Council will have reason to persecute us further. Our 'just desserts,' they'll call it."

"More like 'God's wrath,' Richard," corrected Shakespeare, rising, only to plop down a moment later beside Burbage on the stage apron. "They love to call our misfortune 'the fruits of God's vengeance.' It matters not how innocent we are. Remember the plague of '92. Twas our fault, of course. But don't be melancholy for a while yet. Should the culprit be found, proving that tweren't any of our doing, then we can forestall our critics. The High Sheriff is a reasonable man, especially so when our Lord Chamberlain encourages him in that strange and foreign direction," he counseled.

"But the Lord Chamberlain is, above all things, a politic man. We should certainly have to have the matter well and truly resolved for him to intervene," Burbage answered fretfully.

Ben felt sorry for these two, and the others who owned and operated the Globe. Acting was great fun and great work, but an embarrassment to the families of some. Master Shakespeare's wife refused to live in London with him, staying instead at their home in Stratford. She was something of the Puritan, and those zealots hated players and theaters. Ben's own family wasn't pleased with his decision to become a player. But with the well known Shakespeare as his master, Ben's father, an innkeeper just beyond Bishopsgate, finally gave in and let him leave, against his own best judgment. Even now, years later, Ben avoided going home to visit, so thick was the tension.

"I'll look into this, Richard. Perhaps I can shed some light on the matter," Shakespeare decided.

"Leave it to the constable, Will. Tis his job."

The playwright shook his head and rolled his eyes. "The constable couldn't find his buttocks with both hands. He'll waste no time in arresting Henry Condell. Aye, I'm surprised he's not already here to claim his victim." Shakespeare reached over and patted Burbage on the shoulder. "Don't worry, Richard. I'll hunt this fiend down. Why, I've got Ben Jonson to help me. How could a man go wrong?" And he winked at his young companion.

"Methinks I'd rather it be the real Ben Jonson and not this sapling. No offense, dear boy, but my instincts tell me that the path will be so crooked and hidden that it will take a great mind to unravel it."

"Or one just as crooked," laughed Shakespeare. "But I think you misjudge Ben, my friend. He is a good lad, and he has an uncanny knack for observation." He turned to Ben. "Come, we've questions to be asked and ciphering to do. We can't let the greatest actor in England sit melancholy forever. And Henry needs some time to recover from his fright before we purge him with questions."

Leaving a worried Richard Burbage still perched on the stage, Ben quickly shed his costume and they exited the theater and walked in silence to the jetty below the Globe, on the banks of the mighty Thames, and waited for a ferryman to come across. Legions of barges, loaded with coal and other cargo, dotted the water, riding low and squat against the black surface; a dozen ferry boats scooted in and out around the slow moving ships, hauling their human freight from one side to the other; the cries "Eastward Ho!" and "Westward Ho!" rose from empty ferries. Chapmen—peddlers—hustled their goods to new markets. Across the river little tributaries of human waste constantly emptied their brown muck into the Thames.

"What next?" Ben asked as he turned towards his mentor. Will Shakespeare was a good man. All that knew him agreed. He was neither tall nor short, medium if anything. He combed his shoulder-length hair back from his forehead, and red cheeks gave him a cheery, always happy, look, but he wasn't boisterous. Besides his sometimes biting sense of humor, only one other habit marked him. Shakespeare, when in deep thought, would constantly tug on his earring. After seven years as the playwright's apprentice and another as his roommate, Ben had come to understand the significance of the act.

"Master?" Ben prodded, watching a dog root hungrily into some garbage tossed out near the water's edge.

"Yes, Ben." Shakespeare's eyes had narrowed, but between those narrowing slits lay a sparkle.

"What purpose could Allan's death serve for anyone?"

He looked down at Ben with a gentle smile. "Good question. Tis that which we have to discover." A ferryman glided his boat up to the jetty then, and they boarded in silence.

A breeze blew in over the boat and Shakespeare wrinkled his nose at the rancid odor of the Thames. "There's something foul in the air." But, Ben knew, it wasn't dead fish which offended his master's senses.

❧ ❧ ❧ ❧

"Where did young Hawkins live, Ben?" They had crossed the

Thames and were trudging along the crowded streets of London proper.

"In Blackfriars, Master." Blackfriars was a prosperous section of London, home to well-heeled merchants and others of money.

"Indeed, I did not know that the boy was so wealthy." Shakespeare tugged at his earring a moment, a thoughtful look on his face.

"His father is a trader," Ben continued. "He owns a ship, I believe, that brings goods from the New World."

"We must go and tell his family the sad tidings." Shakespeare released his earring suddenly. "Tis not a task which gives me joy, but we may learn something of this horrible business. Did you know, Master Jonson, that you sound like a court jester with that infernal clanking in your pocket? Why must you carry those things?"

Ben reached into his pocket and produced a ring of skeleton keys. He tossed them into the air and caught them. "Father has a set just like this. Locks are expensive, and an innkeeper becomes his own locksmith if he's smart."

"But you're not an innkeeper!" Shakespeare argued.

"True," Ben nodded. "But there are few locks in London I can't open with these, and you never know when that might come in handy." He replaced the ring in his pocket, where it created an odd bulge.

"Somehow, that doesn't bring me comfort. Lead, Ben Jonson. Much work must be done."

Ben steered the way through the cobbled lanes and alleys of Blackfriars, stopping finally at the imposing half-timbered home of the Hawkins family. The house implied a modest wealth. But a raggedness decorated its facade—a broken step at the door, chips gouged from the woodwork, a shingle missing from its steeply-pitched roof. Apparently Hawkins had not been treated as well in New World trade as some of his colleagues.

A stout man, dressed in fashionable clothing, came through the heavy front door just as Shakespeare raised his hand to knock.

"Ho! Who be this?" The man's voice was gruff, like two rocks scratched together.

"Will Shakespeare is my name, good sir. And are you Hawkins?"

At the mention of the name Shakespeare, the man's plain countenance turned sour. "The same who runs that hellhole called the Globe? Aye, the same man who hath stolen my son from me?" Craning his head around, Hawkins' face lit in recognition as he saw Ben. "Aye, you must be the same. You have another of your ruffians with you."

"Master Hawkins." Ben acknowledged Allan's father.

"No, good sir," Shakespeare inserted. "To answer your charge, I have stolen no one's child from him, not yours nor anyone's. It grieves me to think that you feel such." A glint shone in Shakespeare's eyes as he jockeyed with the man, his voice carrying a mix of gentle honesty and an actor's masque.

"Be gone with you! I'll have no business to conduct with thee."

Ben watched the playwright turn away slowly, as if hurt, for just a fraction of a second. Then Shakespeare seemed to hesitate, facing the angry man once more. "Sir, though your words send me away, I must finish my business, for though you have none with me, I have much with you."

"What is it, then? And be quick about it!"

Ben didn't like the tone in the elder Hawkins' voice. He nudged Shakespeare in the ribs, but the playwright sidestepped the reproach.

"Thy son has passed beyond this vale, friend Hawkins. As my companion here said, he has gone to Elysium. He is quite truly dead." They were sobering words and Shakespeare spoke them eloquently.

Hawkins lost his look of contempt and, as the anger slid from his expression, his body slid to the doorstoop. "In truth? My son Allan is gone?"

"Aye," Ben added. "And he spoke of you at the end."

A redness came to Hawkins' eyes and he rested his arms across his knees, cradling his head in his hands.

Shakespeare leaned forward and gently touched the man on his shoulder. "Be comforted, good sir. Tis a hard blow, but one which you and I must both overcome." Shakespeare sat beside him on the stones. "Tell me, sir, had Allan any enemies?"

The question was bold, but Hawkins seemed too distraught to catch the hidden meaning. He paused for a long moment before answering, his eyes narrowing in the interval. "Nay," he answered. "He is a most pleasant boy, good to his mother, and me. Except in recent days, and he had business abroad late in the evenings. It was most unsettling, when I knew that it had nothing to do with that blasted theater. He told me so, and yet the worry was written across his face. I pressed him, yet he had nothing to say. 'Private business,' he called it. Bah! What 'private business' could a youngster have?"

"And no hint of this secret business slipped from his tongue?" Shakespeare's questions grew even bolder and Ben fidgeted.

"Nay. None. I even threatened the boy, but it came to naught."

"Had he a lover?"

"A boy such as Allan? Methinks not, but thou can never tell in these days. The youth grow up so quickly."

"Aye," agreed Shakespeare.

"But why ask you if he had any enemies? Surely, you are not saying . . ." Color rose quickly in the man's cheeks and anger tinted his eyes again. "Damn'd actors. You have killed my son, and now you seek to dig your way out of the blame. I'll see you thrashed, you Shakespeare. Tis your fault." He stood and jerked open the door. "I'll not say more to you. This house is in mourning." And with that he slammed the door, leaving Shakespeare and Ben on the street alone.

"But Allan's body, Master?" Ben reminded him. "It must be cared for."

Shakespeare moved to the door once more and banged his fist hard against the wood.

It flew open and a serving woman appeared in the doorway. "What is it? The master will see no one."

"Woman, your master made no provision for Allan's mortal remains." Shakespeare wasted no time getting to the point.

The woman frowned and Ben could have sworn he saw a glimmer of fear in her eyes. "The master is much hurt by this turn of events. Someone will be sent. Thank you." She smiled weakly at Ben and then shut the door.

"What can we do now, Master?"

The older man stood silent for a moment. "Did Allan say anything to you of this 'private business'?"

"No," Ben said, "I knew that his mind was elsewhere, that something was distracting him, but nothing more. Aye, just a night or two ago, he missed our card game. But I thought nothing of it, at least not much."

"Did he offer no explanation?"

Ben thought for a minute. "No. Like you, I first thought that it was a girl, but he was quick to assure me such was not the case. Though, Allan could lie when it profited him. He was no different than anyone else. But of late, something was eating on him. It even affected his acting. Just today, I noticed him stumble in his lines."

"Was there anywhere special that you and Allan lifted a glass? An ordinary house?"

"Aye, Master, on this same street, just a bit further down. But what can we find there? Tis just a common house, a place to escape to."

"Ah, good Ben, tis an unweeded garden, and though it grows rank and gross, among its weeds we may find the flower of truth. If he went out in the evening, there's a chance that he went to this tavern. Perhaps someone there knows something."

"I think you expect too much of such a sodden lot," Ben grumbled.

"Have faith, my friend."

As they walked, Shakespeare reached into his pocket and pulled out a small metal object. "Have you seen anything like this before, Master Jonson?" He offered the piece to Ben who took it in the palm of his hand, its shining countenance in stark contrast to the overcast sky, and he studied it closely.

The face of the button held an anchor with a bit of rope twisted from the tip. "Tis just a button, Master, the like of which I've not seen before to be sure. From the docks I would guess, with this anchor at the fore. Where did you find it?"

"Upon the floor, beside the bound Henry. Twasn't one of his. I think we should find the man missing this trifle."

"But how, Master? It seems an impossible task?"

"All things are possible twixt heaven and earth, young Ben Jonson. But think. I have no such buttons. You have no such buttons. None of all our people at the Globe sport such fancies. And the only outsider who has trespassed backstage was the fiend who attacked Henry. Seems logical to think that this button belongs on his shirt."

"It all sounds well and good, Master, but the truth may be of a different element."

"Perhaps, perhaps. Come. Here's the alehouse. We'll sample their wares and see what is to be learned."

Ben had been right. It was a sodden lot, even at this early hour. The tavernkeeper stood behind an ancient wooden plank, propped up by a barrel at each end. Behind him stood shelves of bottled ale and a variety of earthenware jugs. Four or five tables sat around the room, as did their occupants, a grimy crowd.

Ben's nose wrinkled at the smell of unwashed bodies and Shakespeare smiled at him. "The Thames has nothing on this lot," he agreed. "Do you know any of these hellions?"

Ben glanced around the room, squinting his eyes against the spare light. Only one lamp and an open window offered any comfort from the darkness. His eyes fell on one of the patrons, a seamy-looking man with a white shirt, stained with blotches of pink and brown. He wore a beard, pointed in the fashion of the day, but his hair was unruly and one eye carried the pucker of a scar at its corner. "Him, Master, I've seen him here before. Indeed, I may have lifted a pint with him."

"I didn't know you lacked so much for company," grunted

Shakespeare. Another man stumbled into the room, bashing against the playwright as he passed. Shakespeare fell sideways into the wall, regaining his balance only with Ben's help. The drunk passed on by, slumping finally at a nearby table. Shakespeare frowned at the disturbance and turned his attention back to Ben. "Let's see what your drinking companion knows of Master Allan."

The man that Ben indicated was with a friend, both hunkered down over their tankards, and Shakespeare and Ben stood over them a long minute before they were noticed.

"Good sir," began Shakespeare in a friendly tone. The bearded one glanced up once at them and sneered. No answer. "Good Sir." Shakespeare was insistent.

"Have you no manners?" complained their quarry.

"Would that I could pose a question to you."

"Are you from the High Sheriff?"

"Nay," replied Shakespeare. "We are simple citizens, trying simply to find some order in things."

"You'll find no order here," chuckled the bearded man's companion.

"Off with you. I answer questions only when threatened with the jail," warned the first man.

"As you wish," said Shakespeare and he started to leave, then turning back with a serious look on his face. He studied the drunk's features carefully. "Ah, it is just as I feared."

"What have you feared?"

"Sir, I must tell you, no, warn you, that there's something of the plague in your face."

"What? The plague? I feel fine."

"Aye. As you may, but a man of your habits," and Shakespeare reached down and tugged the grimy shirt with a strong hand, "would be hard put to deny the rumor should it ever get started. Why, no alehouse in London would serve you. Rather, they would toss you out on your head."

"Why, it might be me tossing you out on your head." The man

rose with a wicked grin, and Shakespeare's fist shot to the hilt of the sword on his hip.

"And when the constable came to straighten out the mess . . ." Ben inserted himself between the two men. "He might be inclined to ask you about those robberies near Eastcheap." And Ben, too, grabbed a small dagger at his side to punctuate the remark.

The man shifted his gaze to Ben, looking at him for the first time. A frown grew over his unshaven features. "I've seen you before. All right, ask your damned questions and be gone."

Shakespeare dragged a chair over from a neighboring table and slid into it. Ben relaxed and grabbed a chair just as his master began. "Do you know a boy named Allan Hawkins?"

The drunk downed a stiff jolt and nodded amiably. "Aye. If he be the son of Hawkins, the trader, what lives just a lane or two away. I've lifted a dram or two with him, and with this one too, if I'm not mistaken."

Ben frowned and Shakespeare continued. "Did you ever see the Hawkins lad with anyone but this man?"

He considered the question for a moment. "Would the answer be worth anything to you?"

"It would be worth more to you," answered Shakespeare.

An evil glint appeared in the drunk's eye. "And what would that be?"

"Your continued ability to drink in public houses," the playwright reminded.

The drunk growled again and then shrugged his shoulders. "Aye. A man of your age was with him just last evening. They huddled together, there." He pointed to a table set far back in a corner.

"Did you know this man?"

"Know him? No, but I've seen him here most every night for better than a month. Always comes in around eight."

"Is he a sailor?" questioned Ben.

The drunk pulled his head back and frowned. "You're awful nosey for such a small sprout. How should I know how the man fills his days?"

Shakespeare half-stroked, half-pulled at his earring for a silent moment. He held his hand up to Ben, who was about to begin his questioning once more. "We thank you for your time, good sir." The lilt to his voice at the words "good sir" said more than enough about his real thoughts. "Come, Ben. We can visit here another time."

The young actor grimaced and started to speak. But Shakespeare shook his head and turned to leave. Ben followed, begrudgingly, and met the playwright in the lane outside the pub.

Shakespeare, easing his finger into the narrow space between his neck and ruff, pulled the starched, puffy collar away from his neck. "Damn fashion," he grunted and Ben could see where the stiff fabric had rubbed Shakespeare's neck red.

"Forsake city life, Master," counseled Ben.

"For what, my young friend?"

"The pleasures of the country. It is often said that country life is more pleasing to the humors."

"Humph! The idylls of the forest are more perfect in thought than in reality. Never forget that, boy." Shakespeare finished adjusting the collar and brushed a bit of lint off his shaped and formed sleeves.

"Why did we not question him further?" Ben complained as they trudged off up the lane. "Perhaps we could have learned more about this new drinking companion of Allan's."

"No," disagreed Shakespeare. "All we would learn would be of lice and drink. He told us what he knew. There is no more to be learned there until the evening, when this companion of Allan's returns. I'll come back then and see what else can be shaken from this tree."

"Perhaps we can learn from this man, what Allan's 'personal business' was," agreed Ben.

The playwright glanced over at his companion. "You won't be following me. You have lines to study and a public house is no place for a youngster such as you so late in the evening."

Ben gritted his teeth. "I'm your apprentice no longer, Master

Shakespeare. I'll go where I please and drink with whom I choose."

"Then you can remove yourself from my lodgings," Shakespeare said firmly. The pair had lived together for so long that even after Ben's apprenticeship the arrangement had continued by silent, but mutual, consent.

"Fine," Ben conceded with a sharp grin. "Then in my next letter to Mistress Shakespeare, I'll explain to her how you tossed me out on my ear because I complained of your carousing with the wenches."

"You may come along," Shakespeare said with a frown. "But you'll pay for your treachery, you rascal." And he rapped Ben's ear with a heavy hand, sending him reeling, as his frown turned to a smile. But Ben's smile was tight. Moving from apprentice to companion was a difficult process, one which Ben struggled with each day. And as they headed back down the street towards the river, the young actor wondered if the transformation would ever be complete.

❧ ❧ ❧ ❧

A few moments after they had left, the door to the tavern opened again. The man who had brushed against Shakespeare emerged, no semblance of staggering in his gait. He glanced up and down the street, his eyes finally fixing on Ben and Shakespeare's retreating figures bobbing in and out of the heavy street traffic. With a hint of a grin, he melted into the crowd, keeping his quarry in sight, always a short distance ahead.

Two

he waning sun, peeking through the shrouded sky, brightened the sign of the Globe—great Atlas with the world on his shoulder. The Globe sat in Bankside, as the area was known, and only a row of houses separated the theater from the bustling Thames. Down the river a distance was the Bear Garden, where tame bears were baited and taunted for the audience's enjoyment. It was common for spectators at the Globe and the Bear Garden to ferry over from London proper, and traffic was always heavy.

The theater, a round building, was surrounded on three sides by large, elm trees. James Burbage, Richard's father, first constructed a theater on the site just a few years before. Two ground level entrances, to either side and in front of the stage, provided access for the crowds. A flag flew over its heights on play days to let Londoners know that entertainment was to be had for the price of admission—a penny for the ground, a bit more for the gallery seats which rose three stories above the floor.

No spectators filled the doors as Shakespeare and Ben made their way up the lane, and no flag now fluttered from the rooftop. Their ferryman on the return trip had been a stubborn curmudgeon, bewhiskered and bewildered. Though Shakespeare had told him four times to put in at the jetty below the Globe, the old man insisted on delivering them just below London Bridge. They were forced to walk the last half-mile back to the theater, shoving their way through the always crowded streets, taking more time yet.

Emptied, the late afternoon shadows darkening its corners, the sight of the Globe made Ben shiver. A vacant theater was a forbidding sight. On this trip in front of the galleries, there was no crowd to push through and Shakespeare and Ben walked quickly across the courtyard to the stage skirt.

Richard Burbage was in a heated conversation with a tall, thin man, dressed in the latest fashion.

"But, you are not hearing me, sir!" Ben heard Burbage protest as they drew closer.

The thin man snorted and shook his head. "I hear you perfectly well, Master Burbage. But you are not hearing me. This theater must close. The London Council wills it." He broke off his nasal tone and looked about the stage, his angular features seeming to grow sharper still. "Players and plays, evil diversions! Would that I could end it all." And then he turned back to the angry Burbage. "This one I can. Murder on the stage cannot be allowed. Your players have taken their work too seriously. And Master Henry Condell will be brought to charges for this crime. Imagine, killing a young man just to please the audience."

"But you don't understand," said Ben. "It wasn't Master Henry! We have proof!"

"What proof?" the man sniffed.

"In good time," Shakespeare said, putting his hand on Ben's shoulder. "And who are you, sir?"

"I am Geoffrey Middlebury, deputy to the High Sheriff of London." The official held his head high and puffed his shallow chest out as far as he could. "What proof, I say? And who are you?"

Shakespeare raised an eyebrow and bowed solemnly. "I am William Shakespeare."

"Oh," said Middlebury with an unimpressed look, "the writer who fancies himself such a wit."

"I fancy myself only an honest man. It is others who remark upon my attempts at wit."

"The Queen and the Lord Chamberlain among others," added Ben, innocently rolling his eyes. "Why, just two nights ago, a baron came to the . . ." A foot kicked him sharply and an irritated Shakespeare stared down into his eyes.

"A man should learn to keep his own counsel," he muttered to Ben, who sank back, soothing the burning pain in his shin.

"It will take more than your wits to get you and your company out of this one, Master Shakespeare," sputtered Middlebury. "Neither you nor the Lord Chamberlain can argue your way out of murder. It is God's vengeance for your wicked ways. This theater must close. It is a plague and a blasphemy."

Shakespeare smiled softly and tugged at his small gold earring. "We will be happy to close, Master Middlebury." And Burbage stepped closer, his mouth opening to argue while Ben strode forward, ready to join Burbage's protest. "When you and the London Council gain permission from the Queen's Privy Council to order that closure. Until then, it would be improper, nay, illegal for the Globe to comply with such a command. We are not in your jurisdiction."

Burbage closed his mouth and Ben stopped in his tracks.

Middlebury's face colored. He touched the hilt of his sword, but as he did, two other actors in the company, listening to the conversation, moved to Shakespeare's side. "I'm not finished with you, Player," Middlebury threatened. "We will gain the Privy Council's permission and I shall be back with the closure orders before the week is ended. The Queen is not the friend she once was, or had you forgotten about that," he sneered. "Mark my words. You have written your last play for the Globe!" The Deputy Sheriff spun and departed, his sword clanking noisily at his side.

Burbage and Shakespeare watched the retreating figure for a long minute. "He's right, you know," Burbage said.

The energy seemed to drain from Shakespeare's body and his shoulders slumped a little. Ben moved closer to the small circle of men. One of the actors was slim, almost effeminate, and sported a large round earring. The other's face was puffy, from drink Ben guessed; but he was a rough customer and an excellent actor.

"He is right," agreed the puffy-faced actor. "Her Majesty has been in a better humor with us than now."

"We are not alone in that state, my friend," remarked Shakespeare as he continued to stare after the official.

A sudden gloom descended over the gathering. Ben shivered, remembering too well the year before when they had all faced the executioner's axe. It had been early February of 1601, and the handsome, popular Earl of Essex had requested a special performance of *The Tragedy of Richard II.* Burbage and the others balked at first, citing the great expense of production as an obstacle to performance. But the Earl offered to underwrite the presentation, removing the barrier of cost. Then, the Earl of Southampton, Shakespeare's patron during his early years in London, joined in Essex's request. Since Essex was one of Elizabeth's favorites, and Shakespeare offered no protest, the players agreed.

What the Globe company hadn't known at the time was Essex's secret plan. The play contained a scene in which Richard willingly steps down and hands his throne over to another. Using this scene as a springboard, the Earl attempted to launch a rebellion against Queen Elizabeth. Unfortunately for Essex, no one chose to join his revolution. The story went round that he had stopped at a deputy sheriff's house, one supposedly loyal to him, and the official made a hasty retreat out the back door as Essex entered the front. Most of his supporters stayed in the shadows, and the insurrection failed miserably.

A commission was appointed to investigate the depths of the conspiracy and Richard Burbage was called to testify. The Chamberlain's Men were accused of complicity, but Burbage was able to convince the authorities that the actors had known nothing about the plot. They were cleared, but Essex felt the bite of the axe. It had been a tense time, and though they still enjoyed the Queen's favor, the memory of their part in the rebellion, no matter how innocent, could be quickly brought up to discredit them.

"What have you discovered, Will?" Burbage asked finally.

"Not much, I'm afraid. The lad comes from a prosperous enough family. I didn't know that he was of the merchant Hawkins' family."

"If you spent more time in the world and less in your plays, then you would know such things," Burbage chided. "Why, young Ben here could have told you that."

"Young Ben *did* tell me that . . ."

"Somebody has to teach him about the world," muttered Ben.

Shakespeare frowned, and Burbage and the others chuckled. "And if I spent more time in the world and less on my plays, we might not have a full crowd each afternoon," he added. "Question me on Stratford affairs and I can recite them by heart; but London is too big a city to hold my interest for long. My lack of acquaintance with London affairs is of no consequence now. If we're to remain open and keep Henry out of jail, we must find the man who killed young Allan, and we must find out why."

"No truer words were spoken, but surely the constable will clear Henry and get this settled," Richard Burbage argued again. "You are busy enough without having such things to fret over."

"Harrumph," one of the actors cleared his throat. "We can find out about the constable now. Here he comes."

Constable Clarence Parkes waddled across the yard towards them, his feet crunching on hickory nut shells, the remains of the audience's refreshment. Ben had once seen a plate of whale blubber and whenever he saw Parkes he was reminded of the experience. Bright red hair poked in every direction and pink freckles dotted his face. His belly stretched his clothes to the limit as a slightly rusted sword banged at his side.

"Burbage!" The shout came out as more of a cracked squeak than a menacing bluster.

"Constable Parkes, how pleasant to see you today." Burbage was on top of his form.

The red head was shaking violently. "No! No! No! You'll not charm me this time. You've finally done it."

"Constable Parkes, please calm yourself," Burbage soothed the jangled lawman.

Out of breath, Parkes stopped and tried to control his panting. He wheezed and whined, leaning over and placing his hands on his knees for support. Ben noticed Shakespeare watching the lawman carefully with a hint of a smile playing around his lips.

"Burbage!" Parkes finally began. "Why did you not call for me when this murder was committed? Why must I always be the last to find everything out? You've done it now, Burbage. You wouldn't believe the hue and cry that has gone up. Your sins have found you out!" He wagged a meaty finger in Burbage's face.

"Be still, Constable; I was just about to send Ben Jonson here to fetch you. An inquest must be performed." Shakespeare entered the fray.

"Well, of course, of course, an inquest must be performed. I don't need you, Master Shakespeare, to tell me about my job. And you will all be called to testify, to bear witness to this atrocity, this act of heathens. Now, I say, now, where is the murderer, Henry Condell?"

"No man shall call Henry a murderer." One of the actors moved forward, his hand starting for his sword. Ben smiled and leaned closer. He had this vision of Clarence punctured by the sword and dwindling to a skeleton. But Shakespeare grabbed the actor by the shoulder.

"Don't, my friend. Clarence really only meant 'alleged murderer,' did you not, Constable?"

Wide-eyed and red hair standing even further on end, Clarence nodded, backing off a step. The actor relaxed and Shakespeare released him.

"Henry is resting. He will present himself at the inquest, and you may be assured that our testimony will clear him of any wrongdoing in this matter." The playwright spoke sharply.

"But I am supposed to . . ., I mean I should take him into custody, shouldn't I?"

"There has been no testimony against him, Clarence," Shakespeare comforted the lawman. A confused look covered the fat, freckled face and the playwright put an arm around his shoulders and began leading him towards the exit. "You run along and we'll see that Henry appears."

"But . . ."

"No buts, Clarence, trust me. You still haven't caught the pickpocket that plagues our audience. Perhaps you should concentrate on that."

"Didn't I. Caught him right outside, lifting a purse. Tis a month since I've had a report of another. I've been extra vigilant." The pudgy red-head grew defensive.

"Bravo, bravo. The rest of the rogues have probably divined that you were on their trail and chose safer ground." Shakespeare praised the constable, all the while moving him closer and closer to the exit. "We shall see you on the morrow, Constable Parkes. Thank you ever so much for your help." With a final shove, he pushed the lawman toward the door.

"Yes, yes. Just my job you know . . .." And the red-headed constable waddled back out the way he came, shaking his head in confusion and talking to himself.

"As I told you before," Shakespeare returned to Burbage, "you've seen how much assistance the constable will be. He's a bit of a Puritan himself. Besides, there's nothing wrong with Ben and me poking our noses into the matter." Shakespeare patted the actor on the arm. "Trust me, Richard. Who knows, I may find inspiration for a new play. Stranger things have happened."

"Can we be of any help?" one of the other men offered.

The playwright smiled and shook his head. "No. Too many inquirers might drive our quarry further from our grasp. Ben and I will stay on the trail." He leaned over to squeeze his companion's shoulder, but his hand faltered, a distant look in his big eyes. "I still cannot fathom what the youngster could have done to warrant such a tragic end."

The puffy-faced actor stepped forward. "Henry is waiting for you, Will. With Clarence Parkes blustering around, I had almost forgotten."

At the mention of Condell, Shakespeare's eyes sparkled once more. "Where is he?"

"Upstairs, where you sent him." The actor pointed behind them to the three levels rising above the stage. "In his dressing room. He has been resting there until your return."

Ben and Shakespeare mounted the narrow stairs backstage and found Henry Condell sitting, head hung, on a bench in one of the small dressing rooms. He wore an ordinary linen shirt and britches. A tall, slim man, Condell smiled at Shakespeare's approach. The playwright pulled a chair up in front of Condell, and Ben sat on the floor.

"How do you feel, Henry?"

"I've felt better," the actor admitted. Ben liked Condell. He had a pleasant personality and treated the apprentices with more respect than most. And Ben knew, too, that Shakespeare and Condell were good friends.

"What happened?"

"I wish I knew. It was just moments before the scene began. I was standing in the wings waiting for my cue to come on stage. I remember looking around and there was this tall person, my height, coming towards me. No one else was around." Condell stopped for a moment and rubbed his forehead.

"Then," prodded Shakespeare.

"Then," frowned Condell. "Then nothing. He approached from the side and I paid little attention to him, figuring him to be someone's friend, yours or Richard's. I felt him next to me and as I turned, he struck me with something across the head," and Henry rubbed a large red lump behind his ear. "The next thing I knew, you had found me down in 'hell.'"

"You don't remember anything else?"

Condell shrugged. "No. Except that it seems like there were two who carried me away from the stage. At least I think I remember four hands having hold of me. My head was in a fog, thicker than any that caps the Thames."

"Four arms!" exclaimed Ben. "Then there were two of them."

"It would seem so," chuckled Shakespeare. "Unless Burbage, the octopus, was the culprit."

Condell joined Shakespeare in laughter. Ben frowned at the pair. Richard Burbage's prowess with the women was the stuff of legends.

"I'm sorry, Ben," Shakespeare began. "But, if you knew more about Burbage and the woman from . . ."

"I know enough," Ben began, "to know of Master Burbage's reputation with the women." He shook his head at the older men.

"He knows more than we credit him with," conceded Henry. "But, really, that's all that I remember. I awoke when you shook me, Will."

"Does this look familiar?" And Shakespeare produced the button, thrusting it under Henry's nose.

The actor took it out of Shakespeare's hand and turned it over and over. "No. I've not seen this before. Where did you find it?"

"On the floor beside you, beneath the stage."

"Do you remember struggling with your attackers?" Ben offered.

Condell frowned for a minute and then shook his head. "Surely I didn't just cave in, but I don't remember any fight."

"Who else was backstage around that same time?" Ben asked.

"There were many people. Let me see, there was Peter Carew and Robert Armin, and the new lad, Arthur Digges. A couple of the stage helpers ran about, busy at their tasks. Of course, Cuthbert was there, ever vigilant." Besides managing the company, Cuthbert Burbage held the promptbook, the only complete copy of each play. It was his duty to keep the players on track during the performance, slipping their lines to them when they stumbled or forgot. "If anyone saw anything, I'm sure that Cuthbert did. But the apprentices are mere boys," Henry continued. "Surely tis none of their doing."

"None of them are boys any longer," Shakespeare noted. "And

any man backstage, particularly if he had assistance, could have done this deed. Aye, and Cuthbert's duties preoccupy him such that he can't watch everything backstage and onstage as well. But, we'll talk to him, of course."

"But why would anyone do such a deed?" Ben asked.

Henry stretched. "Who knows. Maybe Armin feared Allan as a future rival. Maybe the apprentice boys resented him playing Viola. There could be a thousand good reasons."

"But only one, that counts," Shakespeare said. "These are all that you remember, then?"

"Yes."

"But anyone, Master, who was not on stage at the time could have had the opportunity," Ben noted.

A smile came to Shakespeare's face. "You're right. This makes the reason all the more important. We must trim away the list, but to do so will require a great deal of inquiry." He turned back to Henry. "Had you seen anything in Allan's manner which might have predicted this tragedy?"

"No," Henry shook his head. "But we've been busy of late and not had much time for such observations. If neither Ben nor the apprentices can provide such a change in habits then tis unlikely that I could." His pale features grew even lighter. "I'll be jailed for this, Will. They'll not let me off lightly. Twill be the executioner's axe if the truth cannot be found."

Shakespeare nodded. "Rest, my friend. We'll get to the bottom of this. Ben," he began. "Let's go see if Master Armin is in his room. Tis likely that he would have seen something."

❧ ❧ ❧ ❧

They found Robert Armin in a similar dressing room, hard at work on a manuscript. He dipped his goosequill and scratched it angrily across the page. Shakespeare and Ben watched for a minute from the entrance as the player, his bushy, black eyebrows wrinkling and unwrinkling in anger, crumpled the paper and tossed it against the wall.

"A new play, Robert?" the playwright asked.

His query was greeted with a half-smile, half-frown. "Tis not as easy for me as for you. Some of us have to work harder." Armin stared down his long nose at Ben and smiled sadly. "I'm sorry about your friend, Ben Jonson. He was a good player, the best of his age."

"That is why we have come, Robert," Shakespeare began. "During the play did you notice anyone hanging around backstage that didn't belong there?"

The square-jawed Armin lay down his quill. "Not that I can recall, Will. I was busy trying to keep my lines in my head."

"Tis good that you did. Feste has to appear quick of tongue and wit. A role you always excel in, my friend."

Ben knew that Robert Armin was the best in all England at comic roles. And he also knew that Shakespeare had written the role of Feste, the clown, with Armin in mind. The two were not close, but they had great respect for each other's skills. Indeed, Ben suspected that Armin's respect for Shakespeare's plays edged into jealousy. Armin lusted to have his own plays produced.

"Was anyone of our company acting strangely, Master Armin?" Ben asked.

"No. But, like I said, young Jonson, I pay little attention to anyone backstage. My own performance worries me so that I have little time for noticing the actions of others."

"But, Robert," Shakespeare added. "You were backstage for almost all of the scene before young Allan died. Did you not notice anything, or anyone?"

Armin shook his head. "Oh, I don't know. Let me see. I remember John Lambert coming offstage. He passed me, headed back here, I thought. And the Carew boy and Arthur Digges were lounging, waiting for their cues, coming and going, hither and thither. One of the stage helpers, Harrison I believe, carried things about.

Please, Will," the comic begged in a nasal tone. "I can't remember all their movements."

"You should spend more time studying human habits, Robert," counseled Shakespeare. "It helps improve my plays. I know it will yours. Though I find them excellent works," he quickly added.

A pouting look had begun to grow on Armin's face, but it slipped to a soft smile. "You are too kind, Will."

"Forgive our intrusion, Robert. But if you think of anything that might help shed light on this affair, please tell us. The Puritans are already baying at the doors."

"I will indeed."

They left as Armin took up his quill again and began writing furiously.

"You *are* too kind, Master," Ben noted once they were out of earshot. "His plays stink."

Shakespeare frowned, suppressing a brief chuckle. "You are insolent," he reprimanded, without half the sting the words implied. "You are also absolutely right. But as a player of clowns, he is without parallel."

"Where to next?"

"The tiring house. Cuthbert may have seen something valuable."

❧ ❧ ❧ ❧

"The costume is ruined." Cuthbert Burbage sat on a wooden bench next to a rack of costumes. In his hands, he held Allan Hawkins' blood-stained garment.

This Burbage had little of Richard's charm. Cuthbert was four years the senior of the pair and had a fiery temper. "I have just so much money, Will. I can't spend our last shilling on costumes."

"Tis your gift, Cuthbert, to keep this theater operating. Were it not for your skills we would have been swallowed by our creditors years ago."

The theater manager smiled sourly. "What do you want, Will?

Save your compliments for another. One who believes you, perhaps."

"You are cynical, Cuthbert. And you have insulted me." Shakespeare put on his most wounded look while Cuthbert scratched at his unruly beard; the freckle-faced man refused to trim it, decrying all fashion. Ben knew the two men were the best of friends and at least once daily they found something to argue about. "We are trying to put some order to Allan's death."

"A difficult task, but tis more important to get ready for tomorrow's performance. Allan is gone. Tis nothing to be done now but go on," Cuthbert rasped.

"Master Cuthbert!" Ben exclaimed.

"Sorry, lad. But I have too much to do today to worry about what has already happened. Someone else must trifle with those matters. Allan's dead. We can't bring him back. We must go on.

"You're narrow-minded in your views, Cuthbert," Shakespeare grunted. "Did you not see anything from your place?"

"Only what everyone else saw—what I thought was Henry Condell passing by me onto the stage. Not a half a mo' later I knew twasn't Henry. Voice was wrong."

"But you raised no alarm."

"And interrupt the play? How did I know that you and Richard hadn't made some last second change?"

"Would we not have told you?"

Cuthbert shrugged. "Perhaps. Then again, perhaps not."

"What did you see of the others?" Ben inserted into the pause.

"Well," the stage manager began. "I didn't see much at all offstage. Tis hard to feed you people lines and watch everything else as well."

"Try to remember," Shakespeare prodded.

Cuthbert scratched at his rear. "I believe I saw Carew in the opposite wing with somebody else, the Digges boy I suppose. Robert Armin was nowhere to be seen. Neither was the Lambert youngster. Really, Will, I haven't time for this. We've a play to do tomorrow."

"Not if this matter is not resolved. Did you see anything out of the ordinary?" the playwright persisted. "Did you notice anything about Allan's behavior the last few days? Said he anything to you?"

"Aye," Cuthbert grumbled. "His humors were uneven. He was normally a most polite boy, but the last fortnight he has been most disagreeable, most disagreeable."

"Know you of any reason for this change of nature?"

"Nay." Cuthbert shook his head. "I haven't had the chance to spend time with the boys like I should. The last year has sped by."

"All the years are speeding by," Shakespeare nodded. "We'll leave you to your chores, old friend. Time to move on, Ben. Other questions must be asked."

"Who will be our next victim?" Ben asked as they descended the stairs from the tiring house.

"I suppose we should see if our young apprentices have finished their daily chores or are here yet. It may be that they can shed some light on this matter."

❧ ❧ ❧ ❧

The three apprentices were hard at work painting scenery, a new device with which the company was experimenting. John Lambert, a tall skinny boy with long, black hair and the oldest of the three, was supervising while Carew and Digges, the first short and fat and the second lean, skinny, and unkempt, worked.

"Good work, young masters," Shakespeare greeted them. Lambert turned and smiled broadly at their approach. Ben wrinkled his nose. He didn't like Lambert, or Carew and Digges either for that matter. They relied on flattery, not skill, it seemed to him, to advance. And they had all been envious of Ben's ascent to the list of regular players.

John Lambert bowed. "Tis for your play, Master Shakespeare. *Richard III* opens next week, and Master Burbage has been pressing us hard to help the carpenters with the backdrops and other properties. Some of us," and he looked straight at Ben with a sneer, "have been putting in extra hours."

"Some of you," an older, invisible voicc called from below them, "have idle hours that must be filled." And a sandy-haired man, his long, sad face decorated with an untrimmed, drooping mustache, arose from behind the horse. He wore a leather belt around his waist, and an assortment of mallets and awls dangled from it.

"Harrison, old friend, Cuthbert told me that he had hired you!" A smile came to Shakespeare's face. "When did you arrive?"

"Just this morning. I finished a job at the shipyard and came over."

"I'm surprised you came to work here. Tis not your kind of enterprise. You and my wife have much in common."

"Times are hard, Will. Work is difficult to find in Stratford and, so, sometimes you have to put your beliefs aside to fill your belly. Besides, you and I have been friends since youth. Nothing can change that. And," the carpenter stepped from behind the wooden horse, "someone has to watch over these young hellions. This one," he said, cuffing Arthur Digges on the ear, "would spend his time playing the shell game and gulling his fellows if I didn't keep a watch on him. Quick with his hands, he is."

"Tis all in fun, Master Harrison," Digges complained.

"Aye, and if I turn my back for one minute, I'll find such as this." He looked with a cocked brow at the horse. One eye was blue, the other brown. "Though why anyone would give his kingdom for such a horse, I can't say."

"You've read the play?"

"Tis a good one, Will. But you're capable of better."

"You haven't let me become comfortable with my skills since our boyhood days in Stratford, my friend. Why should now be any different?"

"You knew Master Shakespeare when he was a boy?" Ben asked.

Harrison grinned. "That I did. And these lads couldn't hold a taper to his pranks."

"I'd enjoy the opportunity to hear about those days," Ben said, carefully avoiding Shakespeare's eyes.

"Tis an opportunity you'll never enjoy," grumped the playwright. "Keep your stories to yourself, old friend, or I'll play another prank on you. Aye, and you'll be the worse for it. Can we steal away your help for a moment? There are questions we must put to them."

The carpenter grew solemn. "The other young apprentice?"

Shakespeare nodded.

"I knew that the death would cause you serious problems. Go ahead. Take them. I'll perform surgery on this horse's eyes."

With a jerk of his head, Shakespeare directed the three apprentices toward an unoccupied corner of the theater. Lambert, Carew, and Digges trudged over to the corner, each casting a wary eye at Ben who came along at Shakespeare's side. His change in status left him suspect in their eyes. And Lambert, a year younger, had always envied not only Ben's skill as an actor but his relationship with his former master as well. William Shakespeare was making a fortune as a playwright and actor. And several of the apprentices had hoped that as Ben's apprenticeship ended, Shakespeare would take another under his wing.

"How may we help you, Master?" asked John Lambert smoothly.

"We need to know what happened backstage, in the tiring house, just prior to Allan's death. Who did you see?" the playwright began.

"No one. There were just these two," and Lambert indicated Carew and Digges, "wasting time."

"Ohh, we were wasting time," sneered Digges. "And wot were you doing upstairs in the dressing rooms? Scratching your fanny?"

Ben suppressed a chuckle. Arthur Digges was new to the company, foisted on the Globe by a wealthy merchant just a few weeks before, and he had made a lasting impression on everyone—a bad impression.

"I was readying myself for my next scene," Lambert drew himself up to his full, skinny height and pointed his freckled nose at the ceiling.

"Like I said." Arthur claimed victory.

"Enough! One of your fellows has died a foul death. Does this not mean anything to you?" Shakespeare's voice was sharp, as sharp as Ben had ever heard it.

The three shrank under the blast. Even Lambert, Ben noticed, was shaken by the retort.

"We shall all miss him," Lambert began, but Carew drew in a sharp breath at his side.

"You'll never miss him, John," the pudgy boy mumbled.

"What was that?" Ben snapped.

Carew jumped and his eyes flitted back and forth nervously. "Nothing."

"No," said Shakespeare. "I think it was."

The apprentice collected himself and looked at Lambert angrily. "We all knew, Master, that John hated Allan. He was jealous of him. Many's the time I've heard him," and he thrust a fat finger at Lambert, "say that he wished Allan dead."

Shakespeare raised an eyebrow and he tugged on the gold earring. Ben eyed the now shrinking Lambert.

"John, have you anything to say?" Shakespeare queried.

The thin, sharp-featured boy looked haughtily at Carew. "Aye, Master, I said such words. But they were no more damning than any that Peter and Arthur here said on just as many occasions. I think, even, that Peter had more reason than I to kill our friend Allan."

Ben scowled and shook his head.

Shakespeare ignored Ben. "Master Peter, do you know what John means?"

A wide-eyed apprentice met his gaze. "Nay, Master. I know nothing of this affair, nor did I harbor any ill will against Allan."

"What did you see backstage?"

"Nothing. Arthur and I were swapping stories waiting for our next entrance. We saw John go by to the stairs. And then Ben came offstage and waited across from us at the opposite door. The next thing we knew, Allan was lying upon the boards dying."

"And you had no reason to wish Allan harm?"

Assuming a lie was coming, Ben watched Peter's face carefully.

"He was never very polite to me," the fat boy began, his face twitching. "But I'd never kill him. Tis a harsh thing. Murder breeds an ill wind and—"

"Hmmph," Shakespeare interrupted. "Please. Don't begin quoting me in answer to my own questions." He was speaking to Peter, but Ben noticed that the playwright's eyes were trained on Arthur Digges. "And you Master Digges? Had you any reason to wish harm on young Hawkins?"

The thin, almost emaciated youngster jerked. "Wot? Me? I've only just begun my apprenticeship, Master. I scarcely knew Allan. How could I wish him harm?" His eyes darted back and forth, leaping from Lambert to Carew to Shakespeare. "He was always nice to me," the boy added, almost as an afterthought.

"Allan was nice to everybody," Ben grunted.

A smile drifted across Lambert's face. "He was, was he?" He walked over to Peter Carew, grabbed the boy's pudgy jowls in one hand and jerked his face to profile. A purple bruise spread from the tip of his earlobe down over his jaw. At first sight, it was almost invisible, but laid bare like that, it was bright and ugly. "Your friend, Allan Hawkins did that not twenty-four hours ago."

Three

Carew shook free from Lambert's hand and covered the bruise with his palm, turning away from the others, while John Lambert leered at the expression on Ben's face.

Ben was confused. He looked at Shakespeare, who stared at Peter Carew, cowering before them. "I'm sure he had good reason," Ben tried lamely.

"Perhaps, perhaps," Shakespeare murmured. "What have you to say, Master Carew?"

The fat boy turned two burning eyes on Shakespeare. "It was between the two of us. But it had nothing to do with Allan's murder. I can assure you of that."

"So you say," Shakespeare said. "So you say. What caused this fight?"

"Nothing. Twas just a fight."

"Very well." Shakespeare turned away from Carew. "And none of you saw anything out of the ordinary? None of you noticed the false Aguecheek moving on stage?"

Lambert shrugged and Arthur Digges frowned and shook his head.

"No, Master. Master Condell, or whoever it was, slipped on quickly. He didn't pause," Carew answered, trying to regain some face.

"What about afterwards, after Allan was stabbed? Did you not see the murderer come offstage?"

"I was worried about poor Allan, Master," Digges began.

"We were all onstage by then, Master Shakespeare," Lambert interrupted. "Our attention was on Allan. I doubt that anyone saw anything. It was too confusing, all those people milling about."

Shakespeare fingered his earring once more and studied each youngster in his turn. Finally, after a full minute's pause, he laid his hand on Ben's shoulder. "Come, Ben, we'll leave these to their labors. You and I have other work to do. Harrison!" he called.

The old carpenter wandered back to the little group.

"Here are your workers. I apologize for keeping them so long from their chores."

"No bother." He reached a wrinkled hand over and smacked Ben's head roughly. "Just don't be corrupting this poor young master."

"My head's not a tennis ball," exclaimed Ben, rubbing the side of his head. "Quit whacking it. I'm not an apprentice any longer."

"Ho, Ho! That's a good one." Shakespeare ignored Ben's complaint. "He's corrupted me far more than I could ever corrupt him."

Harrison pulled his hand away from Ben and his tone changed to a somber one. "The lad's family sent for the body and it has been carried away. They'll be burying him in St. Paul's Churchyard two days hence."

"Did you see anything?" Shakespeare queried the carpenter.

The stocky man shook his head. "I was too busy hauling things about back here. And there was nothing to see here but wooden horses."

"Tis a difficult puzzle," the playwright tugged at his earring. "But Ben and I will see it through. Until tomorrow, old friend."

Ben and Shakespeare headed back to the tiring house, leaving the carpenter furiously painting over the horse's errant eye.

"Will!" Richard Burbage's voice echoed across the Globe.

Shakespeare stopped and breathed a heavy sigh. "Yes, Richard."

Ben turned back to the courtyard to see Burbage, a grimace wrinkling his face, walking toward them. The actor seemed half out of breath and sweat glistened at his temples.

"You can't leave yet. Decisions must be made. Tomorrow's performance of *Romeo and Juliet* can't go forward. Allan was rehearsing for Romeo. Tisn't enough time to select someone else, and I'm too old."

"True, true." Shakespeare scratched his ear. "*The Merchant of Venice* has served us well in the past. Ben knows Portia's lines. Tell Cuthbert to prepare *The Merchant.*"

"He'll not like it," Richard Burbage warned, his frown deepening. "He hates changes at the last minute."

"So do we all, old friend," and Shakespeare patted the actor's shoulder. "Come, Ben. Our day has not ended yet."

Excitement started to course through Ben. He had never played Portia, only understudied to Allan during their days as apprentices. Allan. Ben knew the role of Portia just in case something happened to Allan. And now, something had. Ben's mood blackened again.

❧ ❧ ❧ ❧

"Damn your eyes!"

Ben sidestepped quickly to avoid the falling hand. They had returned to the tavern near Blackfriars and a drunken man had taken offense at them, for no apparent reason.

Shakespeare caught the hand in his own and twisted it back. "Be advised, my good man," he grunted, "that I will break your arm without so much as a sigh."

Tears formed in the big man's eyes and he nodded sharply. With a final shove, Shakespeare released his grip and sent the man tumbling back against the bar. "There's a table, Ben. Go get it."

Ben hurried to the table just as another pair, having the same idea, headed for it. With a snarl on his face, Ben yanked his dagger from its resting place and stabbed it into the tabletop, glaring at his opponents at the same time.

One of the men grimaced and reached for his own knife, but his companion held him back. "There's another table over here, Ingram."

"I would be careful of who I was threatening, Ben." Shakespeare sat down and placed a pint of ale before his former apprentice, taking one up himself.

"I saw nothing special about them."

"No reason you should, but the man who thought to take issue with your claim on this table is Ingram Frizer."

"So?" Ben still didn't understand.

Shakespeare chuckled. "You are a dense lout sometimes. Ingram Frizer killed Christopher Marlowe some ten years ago."

"Surely it was treachery he used."

"No one knows for sure, but the inquest jury found him innocent of any wrongdoing."

"A likely story," Ben frowned.

"Never mind Master Frizer. I spoke to the tavern-keeper and our quarry hasn't arrived yet. He'll give me a sign when the clod appears. Pray that the heavens are with us this night, my friend."

But Ben was too busy studying the tavern crowd to worry about the heavens. A lean man at a corner table caught his eye. "Master. Look yonder. Isn't that the man who near knocked you down as he passed this afternoon?"

Shakespeare squinted through the lamplight. "Aye. He's probably been here ever since, sotted and befuddled. Let us use our time wisely." He adjusted his legs beneath the table and sipped on his tankard of ale. "Who was offstage just before this foul deed was done?"

"John Lambert, Arthur Digges, Peter Carew, Henry, Robert, Richard Burbage, and Master Cuthbert of course." Ben clicked them off quickly.

"You have an excellent memory, Ben Jonson." Shakespeare smiled. "No wonder you learn your lines with such little practice. Where does that leave us?"

"That one of those people killed Allan."

"But how, Master Jonson? You didn't do it. Henry didn't do it. Robert knew nothing of it. Peter and Arthur were standing together the entire time. John says he was in the tiring house preparing his next lines. And I stood with Master Cuthbert."

"It must have been John then," Ben decided, taking a sip from his own tankard.

A bemused smile crossed Shakespeare's face. "Why?"

"Because he cannot prove that he was in the tiring house." Ben was getting a little frustrated.

"So?" Shakespeare set his tankard down firmly. "Robert cannot prove his whereabouts either."

"All right, then. I see your direction. Then, we must consider Master Armin as well."

"We cannot stop there," chuckled the playwright.

"Dammit, man, get to the point! OUCH!!" Ben reached down and rubbed his shin where Shakespeare's pointed boot had left its mark.

"Youth should watch their blaspheming tongues."

"You provoked me!"

"You deserved it. Now, listen, if you are going to apply logic, my young friend, apply it equally and without prejudice."

"Very well. But who is this other person?"

"Why, you, Master Ben Jonson. You have no one vouching for your whereabouts."

"Not true." Ben smiled triumphantly. "Master Richard stood next to me during most of the scene, and was there at the fatal moment."

Shakespeare nodded his head in a mock bow. "My pardon, but your innocence has never, seriously, been the question. And your memory isn't as fine as I thought it was. You left out Richard in your litany of actors. But, since you can vouch for his whereabouts, we can safely eliminate him. That leaves us with Henry Condell, John Lambert, and Robert Armin, does it not?"

Ben frowned. "It would seem so."

"There were certain abilities the killer had to possess, certain knowledge he had to have to successfully commit this crime," Shakespeare pointed out.

"Like what?" Ben leaned forward.

"He knew Sir Andrew's lines for one . . ."

"And?"

"And he knew his way about the Globe. How else could he have assaulted Henry, made his entrance, and his exit, so quickly and so unseen."

"I'll grant you that," Ben agreed. He hesitated, staring at the tavern door. "Look, Master, who just walked in."

Shakespeare swiveled and studied the doorway as lines furrowed deep on Ben's forehead. Skulking through the room was Geoffrey Middlebury and another man, both deep in conversation. Ben tried to listen through the noise in the place, but he couldn't catch their words. He turned to his master and found Shakespeare's forehead wrinkled as deeply as his own.

A glimmer of movement caught Ben's eye. He turned to see the tavern-keeper jerking his head back towards the door. "Master. The barman."

Ben watched Shakespeare turn. A husky, weather-beaten man had just entered. He stood still for a moment, scanning the room without moving. Ben studied his clothing. It was a seaman's blouse, covered over by a heavy black cloak lined with a bright, distinctive scarlet. A glimmer of gold shined as the man shifted around to better view the crowd. Ben's eyes sparkled. They were gold-tinted buttons.

"Master," Ben hissed.

But Shakespeare waved him off. "Watch."

Ben fidgeted in his seat. He had to know about those buttons. Taking his tankard of ale in hand, Ben jumped to his feet and staggered off across the room at a drunken gait. Shakespeare reached for him, but his hand fell short and Ben was out of reach.

He staggered left, then right, bouncing off first one patron, then another.

"P-P-ardon-n-n-n me-e-e-e," Ben slurred to each victim. Drawing closer to his target, he saw that the man seemed to be searching the room. Ben staggered further. Just a little closer. Almost there.

"OOooppps!" and he spilled his tankard across the man's coat.

"Ahhh, Masterrr, I didn't mean to get you all wet. 'Ere, let me clean it up." He grabbed a rag off the bar and dabbed at the front of the jacket.

"Off me, you sniveling lout!" The man pushed Ben away with a shove.

"I just wanted to clean it up. Now, be a good master." And Ben went back to wiping, fumbling with the rag at each swipe.

"Besotted fool! Off me!"

The other patrons of the tavern turned to see the commotion, and Ben saw Shakespeare headed their way. When he turned back, the large man was slipping away out the door.

A hand grabbed him by the scruff of the neck and jerked him around painfully. Ben stared into the eyes of a Shakespeare on fire.

"You've spoiled everything, you little—"

"What's the matter Master Shakespeare?" queried a new, self-satisfied voice.

Ben felt Shakespeare's hand release him and he turned towards the voice, rubbing his neck. It was Geoffrey Middlebury, grinning like an alley cat with a fat mouse.

"Can you not control this devil? Has his association with criminals such as you driven him to drink?" Middlebury rubbed his beard-covered chin thoughtfully. "Perhaps I should have you both arrested for inciting a riot."

"You would have your pound of flesh at any price, wouldn't you?" Shakespeare spoke gently, but an edge lurked below the surface and Ben recognized it for such. "The man has a mental affliction which causes him to drink. It only rarely affects him. Why, this is the first display of it in months. You can tell its onset when he begins to foam at the mouth." Ben's leg jerked when Shakespeare covertly kicked it. "And he is particularly susceptible when excited."

"Ohhhh, Masterrr! Don't let them arrest ussss." Slobber drained from the corners of Ben's mouth as his eyes began to cross and convulsions racked his body.

Middlebury stepped back, eyes wide in horror. "The work of the devil! Get him out of here! Now!" And he flung his hand out toward the door.

"Certainly, Master Middlebury," agreed Shakespeare. He put his arm around the convulsing Ben and the pair headed to the door.

Just as they got to the exit, something in a corner caught Ben's eye and he turned, slightly, to see better. "Master!" he whispered. "Look!"

Shakespeare shifted his head around and glanced into the corner Ben had indicated. "Intriguing."

At a table, doing his best to look inconspicuous yet straining to see Ben's performance, sat John Lambert. Upon being sighted, Lambert jerked upright and blended into the crowd.

On the cobblestone pavement outside the door, Shakespeare shoved Ben roughly away from him. His eyes flared and even in the darkness of the street, Ben could see his mentor's balding pate flush. Readying himself for the worst, Ben wiped the remaining saliva from the corners of his mouth. As he did so, Shakespeare's anger began to subside.

"You idiot!" the playwright exclaimed.

Ben's back stiffened. "Stop shoving me, Master."

Shakespeare eyed him closely, but the lines in his face lost none of their sharpness.

The moment passed and Ben's temper cooled. "I was good, wasn't I, Master?" Ben asked finally, filling the pause.

"Good is not the word I would have chosen, Master Ben Jonson." The playwright thrust a finger in Ben's face and shook it. "If you ever do such a thing again without telling me, I'll put you into the Thames as fish bait!"

"Interesting that John Lambert was waiting in the tavern, don't you think?" Ben tried to change the subject, his anger rising again.

Shakespeare relaxed and tugged stiffly at the ruffles of his sleeves. "Aye. It was of note. But talking to the man with the red and black cape would have been more so."

"But his buttons, Master. They were the same," Ben told him excitedly.

Shakespeare raised an eyebrow. "You are certain?"

"No doubts. I wasted a full tankard of ale just to find out. Tis not a thing done lightly," Ben assured him.

"I mourn your loss," Shakespeare grunted. "But it *is* something we did not have before."

"And John Lambert? Surely, the man in the cape came to see him."

"Anything is possible, Master Jonson. But let us not jump to conclusions. Come, we have made enough of a mess this night, and tomorrow is a busy day."

❧ ❧ ❧ ❧

"WHAMMM, KER-WHAMMMM, KER-WHAMMMM!" The hammering of the tinsmiths at labor began even before the sun brightened the haze-filled sky. "WHAMMM, KER-WHAMMM, KER-WHAMMM, KER-PLOP!"

Ben rolled over beneath his rough blanket and covered his ears. He hated the tinsmiths with a passion. Though his father's inn rested just beyond Bishopsgate in Shoreditch, none of the clamor sounded in the courtyard there that one found in London proper. In fact, it was deathly still in comparison. A new sound seeped between his fingers and into his ears, one just as unwelcome.

"Prick me, do I not bleed?"

"Speak one more word and I will put it to the test." Ben threw the blanket back and stretched. "Rehearse on the street. There's no one sleeping down there. Had I a sword, I would test its strength on you."

Shakespeare, dressed in a nightshirt, stood next to the lone table in their room. "If you saved money more devoutly, you'd own a sword instead of a boy's knife."

Ben pulled himself up to a sitting position. "It might interest you to know that I've put aside two crowns for a fine sword. Two more shillings and I'll have enough. Would you consider a loan?"

"Neither a borrower nor a lender be," Shakespeare admonished.

"Some friend you are. You're supposed to see to my needs."

"Was. Was supposed to see to your needs. You're a free man."

When a boy was apprenticed to a man, of any trade, the boy went to live with him. Though Ben could have easily walked in each day from Shoreditch, part of Shakespeare's responsibility had been to provide housing, clothing, and food to his apprentice, something Ben had appreciated. The thought of having to live at home, hearing his father's cutting complaints against the theater, did not appeal to Ben. Lambert was apprenticed to Augustine Phillips; Peter Carew to Thomas Pope. Allan Hawkins had spent some time with his master's family, but since the Hawkins lived just across the river, he spent much of his free time at home.

His apprenticeship had lasted seven years and when he joined the company as a full member, it just made sense to stay with Shakespeare. The playwright had no family in London and he and Ben got along well. Home for Shakespeare and Ben at the moment was this room in Liberty-of-the-Clink, an area adjacent to the Globe. Two small beds graced a pair of corners. A shelf on one wall was overloaded with manuscripts and books. Before the playwright, on top of the table, lay a sheaf of pages.

"You would be advised, my young ruffian, to spend some time rehearsing." Shakespeare continued. "*The Merchant* is not an easy play, and as you heard, Richard and I decided that you will be Portia. With Allan gone you are the most capable for the role."

Ben yawned. "Don't tell John Lambert that. He would take grave exception with you, Master."

Shakespeare grinned. "True. True. But John is yet an apprentice and he is slow. He cannot accept change that quickly. The words do not imprint themselves in his mind. And, to tell you the truth, sometimes his actions on stage seem forced. You, on the other hand, Master Ben Jonson, are a most accomplished liar and can switch roles with ease as the situation demands."

Ben cocked an eye at his master. "Were you anyone but William Shakespeare, I would feel grievously insulted. But I take that to be a compliment from you."

The older man bowed his head in mock respect. "Time to arise, Ben. There is much to be done. Allan's inquest is set at 11:00, and we must have rehearsed the play at least once by then. If we don't, the audience will certainly have its 'quality of mercy' tested. Up, lad, we must be off to the Globe."

❧ ❧ ❧ ❧

When James Burbage and his sons, Cuthbert and Richard, built the Globe, they did so with an actor's eye. Ben was always amazed at the care with which they had seen to every contingency. The interior was designed to accommodate any conceivable plot. Philip Henslowe erected the Rose later, and used Burbage's Globe as the model.

The stage itself was rectangular with a panelled wooden skirt. In the center of the stage rested the trapdoor; beneath it lay "hell," a room hidden below the stage and used for a variety of purposes, a hiding place for Henry Condell just to name one. And, as surely as there is a "hell," Burbage constructed his "heaven" high above the stage beneath the massive, overhanging portico. A balcony protruded from the back of the stage. Just below that was the curtained area for "discovery" scenes.

Three levels of rooms rose behind the stage. The first floor comprised the "tiring house" where actors waited between stage appearances. Hand props were kept here as well as the minor sets that were used. On the second and third levels, reached by a combination ladder/staircase, were the dressing rooms and wardrobe. Most regular members of the company had their own rooms; the apprentices shared a trio of such rooms on the third level.

Ben climbed the ladder wearily, the events of the last twenty-four hours weighing on him. The death of Allan, the two trips to the tavern, and the fracas with the Deputy Sheriff all served to blacken his mood. He barely nodded to John Lambert as they passed on the stairs. The sight of Lambert reawakened his suspicions of the night before and he resolved to pursue the question further, regardless of Master Shakespeare's well-intentioned, but misguided caution. Sometimes, Ben thought, his former master could be too cautious.

With head bowed in thought, Ben stepped into the dressing room he shared with Peter Carew, John Lambert, and, until the day before, Allan Hawkins. His change to regular player had not been accompanied by a change in dressing rooms. Space was tight and Ben, as the newest of the regular troupe, was left with the apprentices.

The room was empty. The others were already onstage. He and Shakespeare were late as usual. A long wooden table sat against one wall and five chairs were scattered about. A rack of costumes rested in a corner. One of the apprentices was detailed each day to bring the costumes for the next performance to the dressing rooms. Ben hung his cloak on the corner of the rack and turned to the long table and his own small station.

He stopped abruptly, shock flying across his face. A note lay on his section of the table, held fast to the wood by an ivory-handled dagger. Scrawled across the paper, almost illegibly, was a single, chilling, line:

"Leave it alone!"

Four

en yanked the dagger from the table and snatched the note up, crumpling it in his haste. No signature. No way of telling from whence it came. Who could it have been? Carew? No, the pudgy boy was frightened of his own shadow. John Lambert? Now, there was a real possibility. Ben snapped his fingers in certainty. He had seen Lambert descending the stairs. Surely the fiend had just finished his dirty business as Ben arrived. The time had come to settle with John Lambert.

Swirling around, Ben ran for the door, scrambled down the wooden steps, and bounded out of the tiring house onto the stage.

He stopped.

Lambert was in deep conference with Shakespeare and Burbage at centerstage, a sinfully innocent look on his pandering face. He was ripe for a fall. But still Ben hesitated. Perhaps now was not the right time.

A smile formed on Ben's face. He folded the bit of paper and slipped it into his pocket. Later, he would show it to Master Shakespeare. For now, he would keep an eye on John Lambert, a close eye.

❧ ❧ ❧ ❧

"The quality of mercy is not strain'd. It droppeth as the gentle rain from—"

"No! No! No!" Shakespeare in his Shylock costume strode across the stage.

"What now, Master?" Ben complained. "Tis the fifth time. Can't you at least let me get through it before you halt me?"

"Why should I let you do it at all? And you, Master Digges, you talk as if you have food in your mouth." Digges hung his head, his cheeks an embarrassed pink. "Do not force the words out. Let them flow, with meaning, with emotion. Speak the speech trippingly, I say."

"Perhaps I should take the part, Master," John Lambert suggested, amusement at Ben's failure flavoring his tone. "It may be too much for Ben."

"In a pig's eye," Ben muttered, adjusting his shirt.

"What was that, Ben?" Shakespeare whipped around.

"I said, 'In just a bit,' I can do it better. Just a moment, please."

Ben walked away from Lambert's sneer, averting his eyes from the faint, dark stain at centerstage, and found some solitude at the edge of the stage. His eye caught the bruise on Peter Carew's face and he wondered again what had sparked his friend Allan to such violence.

"What's wrong?"

Ben turned and discovered Shakespeare looking over his shoulder, a frown widening his cheeks. He pulled the note from his pocket, glanced about for observers, and handed it to his master. "This was on my table upstairs. Stuck there with a dagger."

"And where's the dagger?"

Ben looked surprised. "Why, still on the table. I thought the note to be more important."

"Perhaps, and perhaps not. Never mind. I'll fetch it myself at the first chance. Speak of this to no one."

"But Master, I saw John Lambert coming down the stairs even as I went up. Surely he left it. Shouldn't we confront him?"

"With what? Your suspicions? Hardly. Discretion is the better part of valor, my young friend. And this affair requires us to move quite slowly, and quite discreetly. To do otherwise is to jeopardize our cause," Shakespeare noted, not looking at Ben, but staring at the cryptic message. "Master Lambert bears some study, I'll grant you that. But we must move slowly."

"Not when the guilty party looks you in the bloody eye," grumbled Ben under his breath.

"What? Quit mumbling, man." Shakespeare looked up, an annoyed expression couched on his face. "You're making quite a habit of that."

"Twas my stomach rumbling," Ben lied.

"Well, feed the monster before he emerges to attack us all." Shakespeare paused as a figure appeared before the tiring house. "Ah, Henry's here." He strode quickly over and put a strong hand on Condell's shoulder.

The tall, gaunt man smiled weakly and placed his own hand over Shakespeare's. "You're a good friend, Will. Would that all my friends had your sense of compassion."

Shakespeare lowered his eyes a little and he pulled his hand away. "Don't worry, Henry. Once the inquest is over, you'll be able to return to your life."

"I doubt it shall be that easy, Will." Henry shook his head. "Who's filling my place in *The Merchant?*"

"The Digges boy."

"But he's so new."

"Aye, and totally unseasoned," agreed Shakespeare. "But he's a quick learner. Young Lambert seems especially preoccupied today and so does Robert."

Henry sighed. "Allan's death has unsettled the entire company."

"All the more reason for Ben and I to resolve this matter." Shakespeare patted Ben on the back. "But, the play must go on. Our purses depend on it."

"Then on with your rehearsal and I'll judge its worth."

Ben smiled at the depressed Condell and moved to center stage, to try, once again, his speech of mercy.

❧ ❧ ❧ ❧

"Best get the shackles ready," counseled Constable Clarence Parkes.

"This is an outrage!" yelled Richard Burbage, knocking a chair over in his anger.

The inquest jury had taken less than fifteen minutes to name Henry Condell as the suspected murderer of Allan Hawkins. Meeting at the Red Lion tavern, across from the Globe, Parkes had assembled an odd jury. All looked, to Ben, to be patrons of the bottle rather than the law. Geoffrey Middlebury had sat near the back of the room, consoling Walter Hawkins, Allan's father, and making sure, Ben knew, that "justice" was done.

Parkes recited the "facts" from a sheet of parchment in his hand. "Tis a sure thing that someone else wrote it for him," Shakespeare whispered to Ben as the constable took a great many liberties with reality.

Reading questions from a list in his hand, Parkes stifled anything that any of the other players had to say in Henry's defense and left no doubt in the jury's mind that Henry Condell had maliciously killed Allan Hawkins just to please the audience.

"Another example of the excesses of the theater," Middlebury muttered loudly enough for all to hear.

With the inquest jury's verdict in hand—"We find that Allan Hawkins died at the hands of Henry Condell, player"—Constable Parkes lost no time in taking Condell into custody for trial despite Burbage's cries of outrage.

On the street in front of the tavern, the stench of raw sewage heavy in the air, Ben and Shakespeare watched as Henry Condell, his long face sad and forlorn, was led off in manacles.

"Be of good faith, Henry. This isn't over yet," Shakespeare assured him. But Condell merely forced out a smile and then, towed along by Parkes, he was gone.

Walter Hawkins emerged from the door of the tavern and started towards Shakespeare. But Middlebury, following closely on his heels, snagged him by his arm. The Deputy smirked at the actors and directed Hawkins away from them and down the teeming lane.

"Master Middlebury is a happy man," Shakespeare noted grimly. "With Condell's arrest as a feather in his cap, he'll have no trouble convincing the Privy Council to close down the Globe. And with the Globe out of business, he'll turn his attention to the others. Soon, theaters in London will be but a hazy memory, and Henry Condell will lose his head, literally."

Ben nodded. The jurors had paid no attention to the testimony of the actors. In fact, it seemed to Ben, that they went out of their way not to give any credence to the stories of Ben, Shakespeare, Burbage, and the rest. "It makes our job that much more important, Master."

"You don't know how important, my young friend. I just wish you had taken that dagger. When I went to retrieve it, twas gone."

"I was anxious to tell you of it." Ben hung his head sheepishly. "I'll not be so shortsighted again."

"What will come of all this?" a new voice asked.

Ben turned to see John Lambert approaching. His expression soured at the sight of the apprentice.

"Only time will tell, Master Lambert," Shakespeare answered courteously.

"Well," Lambert sneered at Ben. "If you would spend less time spilling drinks on people and more on freeing Master Henry, then perhaps his sojourn to the Tower would be short. Why, I'm amazed that Simon didn't run you through."

"What did you say?" Shakespeare's tone was sharp and quick. His eyes bore into the now cringing apprentice.

"I . . . uh, . . . said that I was surprised Simon didn't run you through," the young man stammered.

"Who is Simon?"

John Lambert gulped and tugged at the bottom of his blouse. "Why, Simon Fry, Master. The man that Ben assaulted in his drunken stupor last night."

"You know him?"

"Of course. I've lifted a dram or two with him. He's first mate on the *Katherine.* "

"The *Katherine?* Isn't that one of—"

"That's right," Lambert interrupted. "She's one of Walter Hawkins' ships. They've been in port for some time, now. Business hasn't been good, and now this." The apprentice shook his head. "Poor man. My father and he have been friends for many years."

"Where's this Simon Fry now? I'd like to pay him for any damage caused by Ben's revolting performance."

"I'm sure that's not necessary," Lambert answered in a lilting tone, his nose reaching even higher to the sky as he recovered from his own discomfort. "Tis a well known fact that Ben's an idiot. I'm sure even Simon Fry has heard, and he certainly has experienced it."

Ben started toward Lambert with blood in his eyes and his hand on his dagger, but Shakespeare thrust an arm out, blocking his path.

"Enough of *your* idiocy, Master Lambert. Sheath your daggers, the two of you," the playwright said with a scowl, turning after a moment to Lambert. "Where may I find Simon Fry?"

"Hemm—uh—hmm, I believe, Master," Lambert began, pulling his collar from his neck as if suddenly hot. "I believe that Simon quarters himself on board the *Katherine,* even in port."

"How come you to know so much?" asked Ben, an eyebrow rising with each word.

"I told you. Simon and I have shared a tankard before. He's just a man I met in the tavern, that's all. Nothing more."

The innocence and sincerity on Lambert's face seemed genuine. Ben looked to Shakespeare who frowned but made no other sign.

"I have to be back at the Globe, Master," Lambert began. "The play begins at two."

"On with you." Shakespeare dismissed him with the wave of a hand. "We'll be following soon."

Lambert hurried off down the narrow lane, turning every second step or so to glance over his shoulder. Arthur Digges and Peter

Carew waited for him at the corner and together the trio headed into the crowd. Ben and Shakespeare watched them until they were out of sight, lost in the crowded street.

"That should convince you," Ben began, frowning still at the absent figure of John Lambert.

"And what should that convince me of?" Shakespeare was staring off into space, tugging at his earring.

"Of John Lambert's complicity in this affair. Tis curious, don't you think, that he is such a good friend of our quarry."

"True," agreed Shakespeare. "Tis curious indeed, but tis even more curious that the man should be in Walter Hawkins' employ. What would profit a man in having his own son killed? If that is what happened. And, if not, then how did this Simon Fry become involved in Allan's death? If he was, and of that we are not certain. Questions, questions, questions. Many questions are to be answered." He reached over and took Ben by the arm. "Too many to be answered now. But, mark this, Ben Jonson. We are not fighting only for Henry Condell now. Tis the survival of the theater, aye our very livelihood, which hangs in the balance. Come, you must play Portia and present your caskets to the ever-faithful Bassanio. This evening we shall go to the *Katherine* and present our questions to Master Simon Fry. "

❧ ❧ ❧ ❧

The *Katherine* lay at dock at the London wharves. She was a shallow-bottomed cargo fluyt, capable of making runs up the Thames and across the Channel to France and Belgium, and even longer voyages if necessary. Ben had seen many like her. A Dutch invention of recent years, she was square-rigged, shaped like a big, long, fat stewing pot, and was being used in the New World to transport the riches of that realm to England, Spain, and Holland. Many merchants were making their fortunes running cargoes of sugar and other goods from Port Royale, Tortuga, St. Kitt's and the other isles back home to England.

A fog had wandered in off the river and settled around *Katherine's* masts. The white layers blanketed the ship and gangplank, making Ben want to pull his dagger out and slice through. No watchman stood at the wobbly plank to question them and Ben and Shakespeare crossed without speaking a word. The ship creaked and groaned as it shifted on its anchor.

From the dock they had seen light emerge from a single porthole in the forward section of the ship. They headed in that direction now, sidestepping coiled ropes and cargo hatches. Before them stood the quarterdeck, elevated above the cargo deck. A door entered the substructure of the ship directly in front of them, while ladders on either side led up to the bridge.

"Master. Why is no one moving about?" More than a little fear had crept into Ben's eyes.

Shakespeare looked around to Ben and nodded. "Tis a good question, my friend." He motioned for Ben to follow him and then pushed open the wooden door.

The narrow corridor was dark. Only a single shaft of light peeped from beneath a doorway, and that yellow and weak. Ben and Shakespeare eased down the hallway, slowly and quietly. Halting at the door, Shakespeare leaned in close and placed his ear against the wood.

"And wot the bloody hell do ye think you're doing!"

Ben jumped and Shakespeare jerked away from the door.

A man, dressed in tight shirt and breeches and carrying a lamp, was coming through the door from the deck. His hand shot to his dagger and a menacing looked stretched across his face. "I saw ye skulking around the gangplank."

Shakespeare stepped away from Ben and straightened his cloak. "We seek Simon Fry."

The reaching hand pulled away from the dagger hilt and the frown faded. "Ye have a strange way of going about it," the sailor grumbled. "Listening in at his cabin door will not get ye an audience. Knock on the blasted thing."

"Of course," was all Shakespeare could muster. "We were just making certain that he was in."

"Him? In? Fie, man, half of London wants to talk to him tonight. Of course he's in."

"Excuse me, good sir, but why was no one at the gangplank to greet us?" Shakespeare's query brought a renewed frown to the grizzled face.

"You ask the stupidest questions. There's only three of us on board and nothing to guard. Tis a month since the *Katherine* has been to sea." The sailor, still grumbling, wandered off down the corridor.

"Brilliant work, Master," chuckled Ben, a little of his fear subsiding.

Shakespeare cast a jaundiced eye at Ben as he raised a fist to knock. "Youth's a stuff will not endure; you'll be fortunate to see tomorrow." His knuckles fell on the thick wood.

They waited.

No answer.

Again, Shakespeare pounded at the door.

No answer.

"Master Fry!" Shakespeare called. "We wish to speak with you!"

Still no answer.

Shakespeare looked up and down the hallway. No one. He stepped back and squared himself on the door.

"Watch out, Ben," he said and took a deep breath.

"Wait!" Ben leaped in front of Shakespeare. "You go about things the hard way," he grumbled.

The playwright relaxed, a quizzical look crossing his bearded face. "What do you mean?"

Ben reached into his pocket and produced his ring of iron keys. "With any luck, the key to our difficulty will be here. And twill be much quieter and easier than your heavy foot."

"I stand corrected."

Ben fidgeted at the door with a succession of keys. Finally, he heard the mechanism click and the key turned in the lock. A satisfied smile took hold on his lips and he turned to Shakespeare, gesturing through the door with a flourish. "After you, good sir."

Shakespeare adjusted his blouse beneath his cloak and harrummphed. "Yes, well, less bothersome as you say." He pushed open the door; it creaked under his touch.

A single, bright candle illuminated the room. Cramped quarters for a man of Simon Fry's dimensions, Ben thought. The bunk and the desk lay almost side by side with only a little space in between. A seafarer's trunk, the metal tinged brown with rust, lay beneath a porthole.

"No Simon Fry," observed Ben.

"Only in one sense, my young friend." Shakespeare had walked around the desk and was staring at the floor. "No Simon Fry who can speak with us, that much is certain. But here lies what remains of Simon Fry."

Ben squeezed around the desk opposite his master and looked at the deck. Simon Fry lay face down, his arms askew. A dagger protruded from the first mate's back, centered between his shoulder blades. Ben knelt down beside the corpse and pulled the dagger from Fry's body.

"God in heaven!" he exclaimed, twisting the knife around for Shakespeare to see. "Tis. . . ."

"Tis the dagger from this morn, is that what you would tell me?" Shakespeare chuckled. "I guessed as much when I saw the look in your eyes. If it were Master Fry who had a hand in Allan's murder, it would seem that his companion wanted his mouth shut, permanently."

"Master," Ben began, his eyes fixed not on Simon Fry but on the open door. "Won't it be suspicious if the other sailor comes back by and we are here, with his dead first mate at our feet."

Shakespeare raised an eyebrow. "Aye. You're beginning to be a little wiser, my boy. Come, there's nothing more to cipher here. Master Fry will not engage us in conversation this night, nor any other. That much tis certain. Let us cloister ourselves at home and give this matter some thought."

“Some thought, Master Shakespeare?” a voice erupted from the cabin door. “Since when did you pause to give thought to murder!”

Five

eputy Sheriff Geoffrey Middlebury stood imperiously in the entrance. Behind him, the sailor and two other men huddled together in the cramped passageway. Middlebury slipped into the room and glanced at the body of Simon Fry.

"Some gambling debt, Master Shakespeare? Or did you both covet the same woman? Tis of no matter. Your killing days are over." He turned to Ben. "You should have picked another trade, young man. The day of the player is fast coming to a close. Aye, it seems my jail is filling up with them." He smiled with a sneer.

"Take note, Ben Jonson. Crossgarter him and he would be the model of Malvolio." Shakespeare's eyes narrowed as he considered the Deputy. "All pomp and no circumstance."

But Middlebury wasn't moved by the insult. "Soon enough, your prating will be silenced." He turned to his companions. "Take them. And watch the small one; he has a devil in him."

The two men moved forward, one carrying shackles and the other a sword, and began squeezing around the desk to make their arrest. The one with the sword positioned the point against Shakespeare's throat and pushed ever so gently.

"We've caught them in the act, your Honor," he drawled to Middlebury. "Shouldn't we send them to hell where they belong?"

Ben's heart skipped. Shakespeare's eyes were locked with the swordman's, never flinching, never giving an instant of ground.

"Perhaps it *would* be better to save the executioner some time," Middlebury said, stroking his chin in thought.

Sweat beaded on Ben's forehead as he stared, unable to move, at the point digging into William Shakespeare's throat. The look in Middlebury's eyes told him there was little time to act.

At that moment, Shakespeare shifted his gaze for a fleeting instant towards Ben, who caught the flickering in his companion's eyes. He thought he knew what was needed.

"'Ere now, you bloody fishmongers. Keep your hands off me." Ben moved to the side brazenly, tilting his opponent's sword away at just the right angle to avoid slitting Shakespeare's throat. "Get that pig sticker out of our way. We'll have none of that."

Middlebury's hand dropped from his chin in surprise and his two men stepped back in astonishment. All eyes were on Ben, just as he intended, his unexpected outburst capturing their attention.

Shakespeare moved. His hand swept across the desk, dousing the light, and sending the cabin reeling into darkness.

Ben dove to the floor and crawled under the desk. Shouts rose above him.

"What in Heaven's name. . . !"

"Get your hands off me, you boil on an admiral's arse!"

"Where did they go?"

"I've got one here!"

"No, you idiot, that's me!"

Ben scrambled on his hands and knees towards the cabin door. Middlebury and his friends had ventured deeper into the room in their panic. It was still pitch dark as Ben emerged into the passageway. He stood and looked back. Dark figures, grappling with each other, flashed briefly in a shaft of dim moonlight reaching through the porthole. A hand touched his sleeve.

"Let's go." The whispered words were from Shakespeare and Ben followed him through the darkened interior of the ship and out onto the deck. "Quickly, Ben. We have to put a great distance between us. This was an unexpected turn of events, I'll grant you."

Ben looked down and suddenly realized that the knife from Fry's back was still in his hand. A liquid, thick and warm, ran down the hilt and onto his fingers. In horror, he flung it over the rail and, in the distance, a sudden, watery plop sounded.

"No! Ben!" Shakespeare cried. "The knife could have been of use. Think, lad! Think! Too late now," the playwright muttered. "Hurry." They dashed down the gangplank and onto the wharf. A few seconds later and they were well away from Ratcliffe Docks and headed back towards the heart of the city, staying always to the shadows.

Few people trekked out into the night, and Shakespeare and Ben had the lane to themselves. But even in the eerie silence, Ben ventured to speak. "Where to now, Master? They'll be looking for us, tis certain."

"I know a place. We'll be safe there, but we must hurry. You are right, Ben," and Shakespeare's eyes narrowed in the dim moonlight. "They will be on our trail, and quickly. I owe you, Ben Jonson," the playwright whispered to his companion. "I shall not forget it." With that, Shakespeare turned on his heels and lengthened his stride, while a cat, making a midnight run, scurried out of their path and hid among some crates, its eyes glowing in the night.

❧ ❧ ❧ ❧

"Keep your breeches on!" The cry was muffled behind a strong, oaken door. Ben's eyes flickered about furtively. They were only two lanes over from Walter Hawkins's house in Blackfriars and Ben was surprised that Shakespeare had brought them to this area. He couldn't fathom who might live here that would harbor them.

Shakespeare, a look of worry descending onto his face, slammed his hand against the door again.

"Once more and I'll not open the door," the gruff voice muttered. But even as the words were said, the door creaked on its hinges.

A tall man appeared in the doorway, framed by the flickering light of a candle. He wore a rough linen nightgown and had red, curly hair. A pointed beard reached down from his chin and quick, dark eyes scanned his visitors from above a crooked, broad nose.

"Will Shakespeare! God help you. Are you drunk? What makes you batter my door like a madman? And who is this hellion?"

Ben saw a smile wash the worry from his master's face. Shakespeare bowed ceremoniously and waved a hand of introduction from his former apprentice to the glowering man in the doorway. "Ben Jonson of Bishopsgate, please allow me to present to you Ben Jonson of Westminster."

Ben gulped while shock captured the man in the door—Ben Jonson.

With the great Ben Jonson and his namesake surprised to silence, Shakespeare, grinning from ear to ear, pushed his way past his rival playwright and into the house. Left standing on the stoop, the two Ben Jonsons eyed each other warily.

"So you're the beggar making such a name for himself on the stage—with my name," the older man said finally. "Well, don't stand there gawking, boy. Get in before my neighbors join us."

Ben, shocked and mute, stumbled past the red-haired giant and into the house.

❧ ❧ ❧ ❧

"Tis a misshapen creature," the older Ben Jonson agreed as Shakespeare finished his tale. "I know how such things work. I've spent my time in the Marshalsea."

Shakespeare nodded. "Aye. And I did not wish to involve you, Ben, but with Middlebury's sudden appearance at the ship, well, the lad and I have become fugitives and we needed some place to hide for a few hours."

"You're welcome here, Will Shakespeare. Though your plays mock the classics with each line, you are still my friend. I heard about the Hawkins boy's death and wondered what plague it would wrought on the playhouses. Would that I could help you sort out this demon, but I am not in the best position to assist. Twas only last year that I got out of prison myself. I was bitten by *The Isle of Dogs,* you know. And Middlebury is a slippery creature. Tis not an enemy that I would readily make."

"You know Middlebury?"

"Only as you do. His love for Essex was well known, and twas only the fleetness of his feet that kept him from feeling the axe."

Shakespeare laughed. "Aye. Would that he had stumbled on his way. Had it not been for my friend here," and Shakespeare nodded at Ben, "I'd be writing my next plays for the fish feeding on my bones. But, you're right, the waters are muddied in this stream. With a little luck, though, we might be able to separate clear water from sewage."

"The matter is clear now," young Ben interrupted. The older men stared at him. "Tis obvious that John Lambert and this Simon Fry conspired to kill Allan."

"But to what end? To what end?" Shakespeare queried.

"Jealousy. John is as jealous as any man I've known," Ben argued.

The playwright shook his head. "I cannot agree. John Lambert may be many things, but I'm not convinced he is a murderer."

"But the note, at the Globe."

"John wasn't the only player with access to the tiring house. And I have studied jealousy, my friend, and there art two kinds—rational and irrational. Methinks that John Lambert is not an Iago. And if revenge is at the heart of it, tis an Iago at work. But, I am not yet ready to count him out. Too many things are unclear."

"Your master makes sense, boy, though I don't know this Iago he speaks of," the red-headed Ben Jonson replied. "Too many loose ends dangle in this matter for such a simple answer. How came Middlebury to the *Katherine* at such an opportune time? Aye, his part in this affair calls forward a different answer than simple, childhood jealousy. And Simon Fry's death begs more questions than it answers."

"Say what you will," warned young Ben. "But I will still make my wager on John Lambert as the culprit."

"The certainty of youth," Shakespeare said. "Tis a wonderful thing. Would that it was well-founded. If I could keep him from drinking and wenching, he might achieve some greatness; he has a quick and agile mind."

"What I learned of drinking and wenching, I learned from you." Ben reminded him. "And you can hardly use youth as an argument against my theories any longer."

The older Jonson watched them, a smile on his face. "You are a pair, tis certain, but a pair of what, I don't know. Tis there anything else I can do for you this evening, Will Shakespeare?"

"Have you a boy about? I need to send a pair of messages to some friends, letting them know that we are all right."

"Of course. Anne!" Jonson bellowed into the quiet house.

Shakespeare grinned. "Is she still a shrew, Ben?"

His friend frowned heavily. "Not only do you break the Unities every time you pick up your quill, but your silly play almost cost me my wife."

"Twas a brilliant idea. Two fiery people such as you, doomed to be mated against any convention of judgment. An enjoyable task, committing it to paper."

"Aye, and Anne was convinced that I had put you up to it. Nay. She thought I wrote it. But when I pointed out how the author had ignored the conventions of playwriting, she came around to my view."

As he finished speaking, a buxom woman of thirty came into the room, yawning and wearing some sort of linen wraparound. "What do you want, Ben Jonson? Is it not enough that I have borne your children? Would you have me shovel coal now? What? What?" And she stopped in the middle of the room as Shakespeare turned his smiling face towards her. "Oh, Ben Jonson, you'll be in church asking forgiveness before this night's over. Wicked William Shakespeare. Or should I call you 'William the Conqueror?'"

"The lad, Anne, the lad," her husband scolded jerking his head at young Ben simultaneously.

"The lad is no lad and he knows the meaning of 'William the Conqueror."' Ben said, raising his head from the table. He had only half listened to their banter. "All of London knows." He looked at the elder Ben Jonson with disgust. "Think you that youngsters come to maturity with no eyes and ears? If tis so, then you, famous Ben Jonson, have much to learn."

"Saucy little beggar you've raised, Will. He has some of your tongue for certain," Anne chuckled with delight. "You've stayed away too long, Will. Ben has had no one to joust with for a fortnight. Makes him cranky."

"I learned long ago, Mistress Anne, that to spend much time under Ben Jonson's roof was to get nothing done. I have to put food in my belly." Shakespeare grinned at his hostess.

She threw her head back and laughed. "Normal men work at a job and come home to their wives. I'm not sure that Ben ever stops working."

"Such is the life we lead," Shakespeare agreed. "Have you some paper and a quill?"

"Yes, Anne," the elder Ben Jonson said. "I forgot why I called you. Roust that young beggar out."

"At this hour?"

"Aye. He should know that apprenticing is a hard task and that of a bricklayer even harder. Will has a message to send and the boy can deliver it."

She rolled her eyes to the ceiling. "When Will Shakespeare screams, my husband jumps." Muttering to herself, she mounted the stairs and disappeared into the upper level of the house.

Ben watched sleepily as Shakespeare scratched two notes, folded both, and passed them on to the hapless boy. The earlier excitement had vanished, only to be replaced by a numbing exhaustion. He heard the front door open and close on squeaky hinges and then he felt a hand touch his arm.

"Ben."

Opening a blurry eye, he saw Shakespeare leaning over. "Go away. I've died and gone to sleep." The words tasted dry on his tongue.

He felt another presence close to his side.

"Leave him there, Will. He'll stretch out on the floor when the urge strikes him."

"Aye," Ben dimly heard his former master agree. "Tis been a long night. Come, stand me to a tankard of ale and tell me of your latest play."

"You'll not like it."

"Probably not," Shakespeare agreed. "But perhaps it's because they are so *unified,* and therefore boring."

"You hellion!"

Ben fell asleep, despite the roaring laughter of the other Ben Jonson, and the voices faded to nothing.

❧ ❧ ❧ ❧

"Your friend, Shakespeare, is worth quite a lot," Anne Jonson said the following day. "Down at the fishmonger's they say his head will fetch fifty pounds for the murder of some sailor." She had just returned from shopping, and she slapped a fish, wrapped in paper, on the table and faced her husband. "We could use fifty pounds."

The redhead remained silent, as if pondering the thought. "True. But what do they offer for young Ben Jonson?"

Anne smiled at Ben who staggered up to the table as she spoke. "Twenty-five. He's only half as dangerous, though they say he's been corrupted by the devil Shakespeare and took a hand in the killing. Corrupted by the monster's evil ways, he is."

"You are all mad," the young actor said, dropping into a chair. His whole body was sore from sleeping on the floor and he rubbed his neck, reeling back from the table sharply as the tangy odor of fresh fish stung his nose. "Where is Master Shakespeare?"

"Upstairs," Ben Jonson replied. "Readying himself for the day. As you should."

"Readying himself in what manner?"

"What right have you to ask questions, boy?" A hoarse, crackling voice broke across the room and Ben turned to look. Standing at the foot of the steps was a hunchbacked man, a wild look in his eye and a crooked stick keeping him on his feet. His hair pointed in every direction. His clothes were a step above rags and a step below clean.

"Excellent." The younger Ben nodded in approval. "I told you a new look would improve your chances with the ladies. I'm pleased you took my advice."

The hunchback straightened and through the scattered locks of hair, the face of William Shakespeare became recognizable. "You are an arrogant man. I did your family a wrong by allowing you to reach maturity without beating your arrogance out of you."

"Why are you dressed in this manner, Master?" Ben ignored the threat.

"Today is Allan Hawkins's burial. There may be something to be seen at those proceedings. And we can't go parading around the streets of London acting our own roles. Master Middlebury would find that most amusing."

The elder Ben Jonson smiled. "Tis true. It would take more luck than even you have, Will, to prevent your imprisonment."

Shakespeare's features beamed through the disguise. "Twill be fun to tempt the fates. Come, lad, I have a costume for you that suits your sharp tongue, though I doubt you'll find it too pleasant."

Ben's eyes narrowed. "Why do I not trust you, Master?"

"Because," the stout redheaded Ben Jonson replied. "You know him."

And all three laughed.

❧ ❧ ❧ ❧

St. Paul's rose above the London skyline. The church was the premier place of worship in the city. All the best families held their own pews and to say that one worshiped at St. Paul's said the most, if not everything about one's status. The imposing stone visage of the church seemed to guard the noisy town with its own, symbolic, silence. Silence, that is, most of the time. But, as with any church, when a burial was to take place, the family could pay to have the bell rung.

On this day, as mourners filed from the church doors, the bell rang loud and clear, pealing its toll across London. Walter Hawkins had paid his money and all London was hearing of the death of his son.

They walked slowly and solemnly from the doors; Allan's casket, a gable-roofed affair, rode atop the shoulders of the pallbearers. Immediately after the body came the paid mourners and the family behind them. Hawkins and his wife, a short stocky woman, trudged after their son. The wife looked straight ahead; Hawkins stared at the ground. Geoffrey Middlebury, looking quite refreshed despite his late night work at the wharves, marched behind the couple. John Lambert walked at his side, a smug self-satisfied expression on his face.

"Fascinating," Shakespeare remarked. He and Ben stood outside the churchyard fence, looking for all the world like an old beggar and his daughter pausing to pay respects to the dead.

"What's fascinating?" Ben asked, twitching to get comfortable in his dress. The revelation that his disguise was to be a female hadn't suited him. He played girls enough on the stage without sashaying through London dressed as one.

Shakespeare didn't answer right away, peering instead through the fence at the funeral procession. "There's a young man next to Walter Hawkins whom I recognize vaguely. Methinks I've seen him before. And if it's who I think it is, tis an odd thing."

"And who do you think it is?" Ben was tired.

"A young lawyer. One who's seen the inside of the jail."

"Has every man you know been in jail?"

Shakespeare laughed. "No, just most of them. But this young man is known as John Donne, a learned fellow, who was ousted from his former position and sent to the Marshalsea for loving the wrong woman. I had heard that he was handling cases for some merchants, but I didn't know that he numbered Walter Hawkins among his clients."

"Is this of note?" Ben failed to grasp the connection.

"Everything is of note, young Ben Jonson. Some things prove fruitful, however, while others are barren."

The pair turned their attention back to the proceedings in the cemetery. At the rear of the family group came the friends, last of all being the players from the Globe. Ben picked out the Burbage brothers and the apprentices. Two other figures among the players startled him. The faces of Philip Henslowe and Edward Alleyn of the Rose became visible. Henslowe owned the Rose, the Globe's only true rival, and Alleyn was its star player.

"Yes, Ben. I see them." Shakespeare spoke, obviously reading the look on Ben's face. "Allan's fame was widespread. He had a bright future on the stage. Their presence," and he nodded towards Henslowe and Alleyn, "is testimony to that."

Ben glanced away from the proceedings and turned his attention to the street. A young girl, of his age or perhaps less, with light brown hair and delicately molded features, lingered at the fence some twenty feet past them. Her clothing, a simple gray skirt and shawl, implied a modest wealth. She seemed locked on the sight of the bobbing casket, looking neither left nor right, her eyes rigid.

"Odd sight to transfix such a beauty," Shakespeare said and Ben realized that the girl had caught his companion's attention as well.

"Aye," Ben agreed. "And a mere passer-by would have no reason to cry." He had seen the tears immediately, a brief hint of sunlight flickering off the wet, pink cheek.

"Ben Jonson," Shakespeare chuckled with evident approval. "Thou art becoming quick of eye. Why don't we go and see if the young one would give alms to two poor beggars."

Ben looked closer. "Master. I've seen this girl before."

"Where?"

"At stage edge. At the Globe when Allan died. She cried out and when she saw me, she ran."

"Then, let us see what she has to say for herself. Ohhhh, the poor missy is sad," crooned Shakespeare as they ambled up next to the girl, tears still streaming down her face.

She barely glanced at them, her eyes fixed on the casket.

"Is it some relative of yours, young mistress?" Running a hand through his helter-skelter hair, Shakespeare moved in even closer.

"Would that it were," the girl said, turning to look at Shakespeare and Ben. "But what do you care about my grief?"

"Tis strange to wish that the dead man was your relative," Ben joined in, curtsying to the girl.

She flashed a weak smile at Ben. "Not so strange after all. I wanted to marry Allan Hawkins, but his parents would not have approved. I only wish we could have been wed before this tragedy."

Ben's eyes grew large. He studied her up and down. Nothing about the girl seemed familiar. He had never seen her with Allan.

"Here," she fumbled in a little bag that dangled from her arm. "I believe I have two pence for you."

Shakespeare's hand shot out and grasped her wrist lightly. "That's not necessary, my young girl. We would talk to you further." His voice was normal again; gone was the squeaking, crackling beggar.

Ben saw that the hand was trembling under Shakespeare's grip, but her eyes betrayed no fear. She had gumption, in great quantities.

"Who are you?"

"No one to cause you fear. Believe that, above all else, believe that." Shakespeare relaxed his hold. "We have an interest in the death of Master Allan. He was our friend."

The girl studied them closely. When her eyes lit on Ben, she leaned in closer and peered, recognition dawning on her face. "Why, you're a man! Aye, and one I've seen before. You're Ben Jonson, Allan's friend."

"How come you know me, but I saw you only once—at the Globe?"

A tear moistened her cheek. "I've watched many plays at the Globe. Would that I could have missed that last performance." She wiped the tear away and straightened her shoulders. "Allan spoke of you often." Turning to Shakespeare, she grinned in recognition. "I know you too. You're William Shakespeare. And I've seen you on stage many times. Allan talked of both of you a great deal. But his parents so objected to our union that he kept our love a secret, from most."

"From me especially, it would seem," Ben grumbled. "But where did you meet and when? I was with Allan most every day."

"More importantly," Shakespeare interrupted. "What is your name, dear girl?"

"Susanna Mayo." And she began to curtsy. He stopped her with a hand.

"Please, Susanna, doing honor to a beggar such as I would be out of joint."

"And why are you dressed so?"

Ben liked the frankness of her speech. She was plain-spoken if nothing else.

"We have been accused of the death of Simon Fry by his royal Puritanness, Geoffrey Middlebury, who stands over there consoling Walter Hawkins. We thought it best to conceal our presence."

She nodded. "I had heard of Simon Fry's death and mourned not. He was a scoundrel, one step removed from a highwayman. Allan hated him with a fury I've never seen."

"Why?"

"Simon was the muscle behind Walter Hawkins's plans. Walter Hawkins is something of a Puritan as well, and he was pushing Allan to commit some treachery at the Globe. Aye, some treachery like that which took Allan's life. The pressure was great. Allan carried more than one mark from Simon Fry at Walter Hawkins's command."

"The father had him beaten that severely?" Shakespeare frowned.

"Walter Hawkins isn't, . . . I— I mean . . . wasn't, Allan's true father."

Six

en and Shakespeare gaped in unison.

"You told me nothing of this," Shakespeare turned to his skirted companion.

"How was I to know?" Ben shrugged.

"Only a few remember," Susanna said. "Allan's real father was the brother of Walter Hawkins. When the father died, the brother rushed in to marry the newly eligible widow. Allan was but two years old and he has—had—only a scarce memory of his father. Twas Allan's father who built the shipping business. Walter has done nothing but cause its decline. Indeed, rumor has it that Master Hawkins has been consorting with pirates on the Spanish Main in hopes of trying to recoup some of his lost fortune."

A man, properly hosed, ruffled, and doubleted, eyed the trio warily as he passed on the lane, keeping his eye on them even as he moved several feet past.

Ben nudged Shakespeare who turned his head towards the observer. The playwright frowned.

"Mistress Mayo, is there somewhere else we could talk. Such as us, conversing with a young lady, brings attention we can ill afford."

Her blue eyes glittered damply as she nodded. "Follow me, but not too closely. My parents live in this area."

The trio moved into the residential area adjacent to St. Paul's.

Walking past half-timbered houses and a scattering of thatch-roofed buildings, Susanna kept a twenty-foot lead as Ben cavorted around Shakespeare, acting completely the role of street urchin. No one, among the throngs on the road, paid any attention to the pair.

Ben halted in his capering long enough to realize that Susanna had led them in front of a row of abandoned houses, something not often seen in the overcrowded streets of London. She looked neither left nor right, merely turned into one of the forlorn structures as if she had simply been out for a walk and was returning home. The young actor glanced about, noting that the lane was virtually empty. Then he saw that Shakespeare had already followed the girl inside and he scampered to catch up, tripping over his skirt in the process.

A hazy grey light filtered through the shuttered windows and brightened the room. Ben blinked a couple of times, trying to adjust to the dim light. Someone had set up a table in the middle of the floor and two chairs were pushed together nearby. In the center of the table sat a single taper, melted down almost completely.

"What is this place?" Ben asked, his voice echoing off the walls.

"Tis where Allan and I stole our time together." The words were spoken somberly. Susanna Mayo kept her back to the pair for a second. Turning around at last, she smiled weakly. "I'm sorry. But tis a hard blow to take. I loved him very much."

Ben felt a slight flush draw over his face like a curtain. Allan had had a way with maidens that his older friend couldn't claim. This new evidence of that charm irritated Ben. Suddenly finding himself slouched, he straightened. "Allan was a good man. We all loved him."

"Aye, Mistress Mayo. What Ben says is true. Allan was indeed our friend, one we shall miss greatly. But, if I might, I would like to hear more of this treachery."

Susanna smiled again. "I'll tell you all I know." She sat down in one of the chairs and rested an arm on the table. "Allan loved the stage. He wanted no other work to fill his days. But, a fortnight ago, his uncle came to him and asked a favor of him. Since his father died so young, Allan wanted mightily to please his step-father, a man," she frowned, "who knows not how to be pleased. So Allan listened, eagerly at first. Walter Hawkins asked him to wound one of his fellows during a performance at the Globe."

"But why would Walter Hawkins want a player harmed?" Ben couldn't see the logic.

"Twas Allan's question exactly. Walter Hawkins was evasive at first, but he finally admitted to Allan that some wealthy people were willing to buy him out of debt if he could arrange for Allan to nick one of the players with his sword."

"What good could come of that?" Ben asked.

"None," Shakespeare agreed. "At least for the Globe."

"Wait," Susanna held up a hand. "Hold your thoughts. There's more. After committing this deed, Allan was to claim that you, Master Shakespeare, and Master Richard Burbage had forced him to do it for the crowd's pleasure."

"Tis becoming clearer," Shakespeare pulled thoughtfully at his earring. "Such an act would. . . ."

"Why, 'twould prove that all that the Puritans say about us is true," finished Ben, irritation flooding his voice.

"Very good, Master Jonson," Shakespeare agreed. "Go on, Susanna."

"Allan refused. And Walter Hawkins begged and pleaded. He tugged at Allan's loyalty to his family. Aye, he even invoked the name of Allan's real father. But, as much as Allan loved his family, he didn't want to hurt one of you, nor the Globe either. Then. . . ." her voice drifted into a soft whisper.

"Then, what, Mistress. This story must be told." Shakespeare's prodding was gentle, with a voice almost as soft as the girl's.

Susanna breathed deeply, and Ben watched her hand catch a moistness at the corner of her eye. "Then, Walter Hawkins told Allan that he would arrange for our marriage straightaway—if Allan would do as he asked. We had waited so long. Allan came to me here and told me of it. He was willing to do it, but I would have no part of a marriage created by spilt blood. I knew that Allan would someday regret what he had done.

"So, he went back to Walter Hawkins and told him no once more. Then, Master Hawkins' true heart was revealed. He told Allan that he would have me badly hurt, killed even, if Allan did not do what he asked. Simon Fry brought the message to Allan three nights ago. It was a horrible scene that night. Allan sent to me late at night and I had to slip from my window and make my way here alone."

"What did he say?" Ben strode forward anxiously.

"He wouldn't tell me all that was said. He was frightened that night, tis true. Frightened as I've never seen him. Kept mumbling things—Essex and James—never connecting the two. But those two things need no connection. It became clear that Simon Fry had told him much. Some wealthy Puritans on the London Council were behind Walter Hawkins."

Ben watched as Shakespeare nodded, seemingly unsurprised.

"And?" the playwright questioned.

"We decided to run away. Twas obvious that Allan could find no peace, even in his own home. We were to meet after the performance at the Globe the next day. Allan told only his mother. He was going to come to you, Master Shakespeare, and tell you everything." Susanna lowered her eyes. "And ask for help."

"Help I would have gladly given," Shakespeare smiled grimly.

"But, twas not to be. The next day, his final performance became just that. He was killed." She made the point blunt, yet Ben felt it sear through his stomach.

Shakespeare had continued to nod his head through the questioning. Something in the older man's eyes told Ben that he was making a mental record of all being said, missing neither words nor nuance. "This is all you know of the affair?"

Her eyes flashed a hint of anger. "Understand, Master Shakespeare, I want Allan's murderer to pay as much as you do. Had I more knowledge, I would gladly give it."

"Of course, dear girl. I was just making sure." The playwright stood and crossed his arms, a thoughtful look seizing his face. After a few moments of silence, he turned to Ben. "Where does that leave us, Master Jonson? We have learned much today."

Ben's eyebrows wrinkled together as he concentrated. "She answers several questions. Simon Fry was obviously threatening Allan that night. And the next day he carried out his threats."

"You say then that Fry made himself up as Aguecheek and ran Allan through?"

"Tis possible."

"Tis unlikely. The false Aguecheek knew the lines; twas only the movements which caused him hesitation. Where would Simon Fry learn the lines? *Twelfth Night* is too new. No pirated quartos are on the streets. I keep up with such things. And Fry is too tall." Shakespeare stroked his beard a moment. "I don't doubt, mind you, that Simon Fry helped the murderer dispose of Master Henry. But he was an accomplice. I want the man who gave Allan a diet of steel, and I want the man who ordered it."

"I want some order to this mess," Ben said, hanging his head. "Too many 'can't be's' and not enough 'can be's'. Still," and he raised up. "There's no doubt now that John Lambert is the man. He fits the bill too handily and tis obvious that he walks hand in hand with Walter Hawkins and Deputy Middlebury."

Shakespeare shook his head. "Too many things are 'obvious' to you, and tis the obvious which we must avoid if we are to sort out this affair. It does get stickier by the minute. That I will give you. But there is less unclear now, if the brew is thicker. We know the probable 'why' of Allan's death now. Tis the 'who' which must occupy our time, and too many people had the opportunity to plunge their sword into Allan to settle on one right now. Though," and Shakespeare smiled his famous smile. "John Lambert's choices in companionship leave much to be desired. And he is not clear of suspicion. But we must not be narrow-minded. Remember that, always."

Ben frowned. "And while we're remembering your famous dictums, the killer is laughing at us."

"You are impatient. Twill cause you problems."

"Impatience can sometimes be a virtue, Master Shakespeare." Susanna Mayo entered the discussion. "I would bring Allan's murderer to answer for his crime this minute were it in my power. Without such devotion to the cause, I fear chances of your success are slim."

Ben studied the firm set to her jaw, and her erect stance. No wonder Allan had kept her to himself. She was an enchantress. Of that, there was little doubt. "What shall we do next, Master?" Ben changed the subject.

Shakespeare paused and eyed his former apprentice carefully. "Methinks a change of costume is in order."

With a whisk, Ben pulled the dress over his head, revealing his normal clothes beneath. The dress had neatly covered the other garments. He smiled and tossed the clothing in a corner.

"But won't he be recognized?" Susanna asked.

"Not that many people know him, Mistress Mayo," Shakespeare assured her.

Ben frowned in aggravation. "Now what?"

"You will accompany our new friend home. A respectable girl can't be seen in the lane with a street urchin. But, a young lady taking a walk with her older brother is another matter. See that she arrives safely. And stay away from your normal haunts."

"But, Master . . ." Ben protested. He didn't like the idea of being saddled with the girl. At another time perhaps, but now was not that time.

Shakespeare held up a hand. "No buts. I will go back to our sanctuary, after a few stops, and make further plans. Yes, and cogitate on this problem a while longer. Meet me there when your errand is finished."

"But, Master!"

"Go, you young hellion! Now!" Shakespeare's eyes flared.

"This affair has turned his temper," Ben muttered as they emerged onto the lane. He straightened his shirt and started off down the way, Susanna now hurrying to keep up.

"You're an odd one, Ben Jonson," she said, drawing even with him.

"And how's that?" He avoided looking at her.

"You're supposed to walk me home, not make me run after you the whole way." She was almost out of breath.

"You're supposed to keep up."

"Why are you angry?"

And he was. He knew his mood was wrong. Something irritated him and he didn't know the cause.

"Twas wrong of Allan not to tell me of you." He spoke the words without thinking them first.

"Allan cared about you deeply, Ben Jonson. You were his best friend."

"All the more reason."

"Perhaps he had more reason to keep me a secret from you."

"We were friends; nay, he had no reason to keep you from me. We gambled together. Drank together. Aye, we toasted the maidens together. Why, when I finished my apprenticeship, he gave me this," and Ben displayed his dagger.

"You make hasty decisions," she scolded him. "Allan was very jealous, and that was enough reason for him."

"He had little to fear from me." Ben intentionally kept his eyes from lighting on her. Staring straight ahead, he focused on the crowds in the street before him. "How close to St. Paul's do you live?"

Susanna sighed. "Not far. I'll show you."

She pointed out a direction and they walked on in silence, looking for all the world like a brother and sister out for an afternoon errand, her occasional comments greeted only by Ben's obstinate grunts.

Soon they drew abreast of St. Paul's. The giant spire rose high over London and Ben sucked in his breath sharply at the sight.

"Ben!"

The exclamation broke his reverie and he glanced at Susanna. Her hand was pressed against her mouth and she looked down the crowded lane towards the church gate.

"Is that not the apprentice, John Lambert?"

Ben looked where she indicated and sure enough, there, next to the fence of St. Paul's, stood the spindly Lambert. He was talking in an animated fashion to none other than Geoffrey Middlebury and Walter Hawkins. The Deputy Sheriff patted Lambert's arm paternally and Hawkins smiled at the apprentice.

The noise in the street was too loud for Ben to hear the conversation, but he could tell by the exaggerated way Lambert was mouthing his words that it was quite a performance. Ben turned away, nauseated by the sight, and recognized Peter Carew and Arthur Digges lounging against the church fence. The other mourners had evaporated into the street crowd.

Looking back to Lambert, he noted that Hawkins had drawn the young apprentice off to the side and they were engaged in a serious conversation. Middlebury was conferring with another man. A fine sheen of sweat broke across Ben's forehead as he realized that it was one of the men from the *Katherine* the night before.

"Don't gawk," Susanna whispered.

Ben realized that he was staring a little too obviously and he moved down the lane, with Susanna at his side, stopping finally behind a horse hitched to a wooden cart. The horse shuffled restlessly before a wheelmaker's shop and Ben stroked its back to calm it. Using the animal for a shield, he kept his eyes trained on the men.

Hawkins patted Lambert on the back and slipped something in his pocket. The apprentice's smiling eyes never left the older man's face and they shook hands. Middlebury came back over and took Lambert's hand in his. Lambert parted company from the men and headed towards Carew and Digges at the fence.

The skinny Digges and his fat companion straightened as Lambert approached. Digges jostled against Lambert playfully and Carew punched the older boy in the arm. Lambert said something and they all laughed and started down the lane towards Ben and Susanna. Ben heard a hint of the joke across the breeze as they drew closer, and he bent low behind the horse, pulling Susanna down with him.

"It doesn't hurt to have lots of friends," Lambert cracked.

"Yeah." Carew was smiling. "As long as Master Burbage doesn't find out who your new friends are."

"I was merely consoling Allan's father," Lambert replied with a smirk.

"Come," Lambert continued. "I've an appointment to keep later."

The trio continued down the lane and Ben straightened.

"How far are we from your home?"

She frowned. "Not far. Why?"

"Get there," Ben ordered with a firm set to his jaw. "I'm going to follow this skunk in player's clothing and get the proof I need. If Master Shakespeare can't see the guilt written all over John Lambert, I can."

"Ben Jonson, you'll be taken and imprisoned."

He shook his head. "As Master Shakespeare pointed out, not that many people in London know who I am."

"Aye, I'll agree to that, but John Lambert and his friends do," she reminded him.

He paused and considered the danger. But after a second's hesitation, he made his decision and squared his shoulders. "Tis a chance I'll have to take."

"Not without me," came the declaration.

Ben spun. "I'll be damned if you will."

She stared at him with an equally firm set to her face. "Probably, but Allan Hawkins meant much to me and I'll see his killer given the axe if I can. You can't go by yourself. I can be of use to you."

"In a pig's eye."

She faced him and locked her eyes on his. "I've had my say, Ben Jonson. Lead on."

For just a second, a mere fraction of a moment, Ben was lost in those eyes. But it was long enough. He bowed his head. "All right. Tis against my better judgment, but there'll be no arguing with you. I see that. Just listen to me and do what I say."

"If it makes sense." Susanna qualified the condition.

"Tis a mistake." Ben shook his head.

"Twill be if you don't get going. They're almost out of sight."

"Follow me, then. And may God preserve us both." Ben searched the crowd for the dwindling figures of Lambert, Carew, and Digges. They were just turning the corner a block away. "Come, time's awasting."

With a shake of her head, she followed slowly. "We should fetch your master, Ben Jonson. I've a feeling we'll both regret this."

"Make up your mind."

"You throw caution to the wind."

"Then go home."

She stared at him for a second, a strong grimace shaping her face. "Lead on."

They emerged onto the lane and Ben searched the bobbing heads on the crowded street. Damn the girl and her hesitation! Lambert and his friends had disappeared. No. Wait. There, just beyond Fielding's Printers. John Lambert's pointed head appeared and next to it the round melon of Peter Carew. Three streets ahead.

"Be quiet and do exactly as I say," he cautioned her once more.

"Only if it makes sense," she warned him.

From their direction, east on Watling Street, Ben guessed that the trio was headed for a tavern. The afternoon performance at the Globe had been cancelled in mourning over Allan's death and they would have nothing better to do.

"What are we looking for?" Susanna hissed.

"I don't know. But I heard Lambert mention an appointment later in the day. Perhaps it will be with his masters, Hawkins and Middlebury. If we can keep them in sight, I am sure some slip will occur."

"The foundation for your surety seems built on shifting sands."

"Have you a better plan?" He was tired of her complaints.

"No," she grudgingly admitted.

"Then, be silent."

And for once she obeyed.

But the only silence about them was hers. Everywhere else, up and down the street, came the clattering and banging of silversmiths and the calling of merchants hawking their wares. It was late afternoon, and the haze in the sky signaled the onset of dusk, but London was at fever pitch.

Even in February, the city had a heat of its own and Ben felt the glow as they whisked in and out of the crowd, keeping the trio in sight. London was his city and he loved its noise, for all his complaints. Always, always there was something going on. Hammers beat on one corner. Pots clanked and banged on a second. Tubs were hooped on a third. And water-tankards ran at full tilt on a fourth.

People gathered on every corner. Ben had seen so many folks buck and push up against buildings that the walls came crashing down. Some structures had posts set against them to keep the crowd from shouldering the walls down. Fat porters carried bundles from shops to houses and from shop to shop. Tradesmen danced their peculiar dance as they goaded customers into their thatch-roofed shops, never remaining still it seemed for a single instant.

"Where are they going?" Susanna broke her silence after several minutes of dodging people.

"I'm not sure. Could be that they're headed to a tavern."

"Of that I've no doubt. But will they not mourn their fellow for a longer time?"

"Why?" Ben asked. "They didn't like Allan, and his death just means larger roles for them. Tis likely that they'll celebrate." He strained his neck trying to keep them in sight.

"Even Peter Carew? I would think him so fat that he could hope for just a few roles at best."

"Peter has a comic side to his nature, and he plays well in the comedies, but there is no drama to his performance. He yearns for something else. I'm not sure what."

"A lean and hungry look, perhaps," Susanna quipped.

Ben scowled. "You and Master Shakespeare would get along well together. Your wit is overpowering." He paused, sidestepping a beggar clutching at his feet. "Peter has a need to be liked by his fellows, I think. But so do we all."

"True." Susanna nodded. "You have a telling eye, Ben Jonson."

Ben didn't answer. His telling eye was fixed on the figures in the crowd ahead. They had stopped where Cannon Street, for Watling had turned into that lane, met Gracechurch Street and Ben and Susanna had drawn far closer than he had wished. Damn all this conversation, he thought.

He shifted around an overgrown apprentice lugging a tub hoop down the lane, and his heart skipped a beat. Arthur Digges was staring straight at him!

Ben froze in his tracks, unsure of what to do. But the apprentice's expression didn't change. Digges turned back to John Lambert and shouted something at him, and Ben's breath returned.

The trio was arguing. From the sounds of it, they were disagreeing over which tavern to visit. Lambert was holding out for the Cross Keys and Digges wanted to go on north to the Bull. Carew seemed to be siding with Digges, but it was hard for Ben to tell.

"What's the matter?" Susanna had slipped closer to him and he could smell her scent.

Without answering he pushed her towards the cover of a silversmith's shop in a small alcove.

"Quit shoving me around!"

"Hush, girl. They almost saw us. We'll have to be smarter in our following." Ben leaned back against the building, keeping an eye trained on the still-arguing trio, and let his thumping heart calm.

"Tis certain that I'm not leading," Susanna muttered.

Ben looked at her, a frown growing on his face. "Tis certain that if you'd listened to me, I'd not be having to drag you along, taking chances I'd not normally take."

"And tis just as certain that if you'd pay less attention to me and more to your quarry, you'd see that they've settled their dispute."

Whipping around, Ben glimpsed the three figures blurring into the crowd. Damn the girl and her blasted interference!

He grabbed Susanna by the hand and dragged her into the river of people flowing north, towards Bishopsgate, and the English countryside. A monk, from one of the priories outside the city walls Ben supposed, waddled in the lane and the pair took advantage of the man's bulky brown robes to conceal themselves from their prey.

Poking his head over the shoulder of the monk, who was blissfully unaware of Ben and Susanna, the young actor watched as Lambert led the other two into the Cross Keys Inn. Ben heard Lambert say something about buying the first round. So, Lambert had won out, at a price.

Ben abandoned the monk's camouflage and stood in the middle of the lane. Susanna stood by his side and grimaced.

"Now what?" she asked.

"It poses a pretty problem," he agreed. "I must hear what goes on in there, but I cannot let them see me. A difficult task in such a small room."

He moved to the side of the street, jumping over a dog lapping at garbage, and leaned against a stone building. The inn sat across from him. A barrel-maker's shop sat to the right of the Cross Keys; a narrow alley ran on its left side. As he studied the building, a light began flickering in the front window. Dark was settling in around the city. Night would fall soon.

"Have you a solution to your pretty problem?" she prodded.

Ben ignored her, watching instead a slender, balding man emerge from the alley with a pan of table scraps which he tossed towards the street. A grimy leather apron circled his waist and a permanent sneer was affixed to his lip. He grimaced at the people in the streets, none of whom turned into the inn door.

A thought struck Ben and he straightened.

"Stay here," he ordered.

Susanna raised her eyebrows. "I will not."

"Just do it." The order was terse.

Ben left the girl gaping and trotted across the lane. "Your pardon, Master."

The sneering man looked up. "Wot would ye be wantin' with me?"

"Don't be in such an ill humor." Ben reached into a pocket and pulled out a coin. Tossing it into the air, he smiled at the innkeeper. "I need a favor."

"Tis that a crown?" A leer replaced the sneer.

"Twill be if I might have a word with you." Ben glanced at the busy street. "Somewhere less public."

The innkeeper jerked his head towards the alley and Ben followed him back. "Now, what will bring me that crown, and be quick about it."

"Just let me slide behind the bar."

"Let you barkeep?"

"No, let me hide there, out of sight. I have some friends inside and I would like to listen to their talk."

"Aye. It can be arranged. But ye must keep your head down and enter when I do." The gleam of the crown was still in the innkeeper's eye. He started inside, but Ben grabbed his arm.

"One other thing. I have a girl and I can't leave her in the street. Can she stay in the kitchen?"

"I'll not be having a harlot in my place," the bald man warned.

Ben's hand shot to the innkeeper's throat and the fingers clamped down hard. "She's a respectable girl. Don't forget it."

The man wrenched free and coughed, rubbing his throat. "Strong for such a youngster." He looked closely at Ben and his eyes brightened. "I've seen you before. Aye, here at my own inn. You're Will Shakespeare's apprentice, ain't you?"

A chill grabbed the pit of Ben's stomach and he backed off a step.

"Hold on, boy. I thought as much when I saw you. I'll not be likely to turn you in," the innkeeper rasped.

"I *was* his apprentice. But now, I'm part of the company."

The innkeeper nodded. "When Shakespeare acted his plays here, I made more money in a day then I do now in a week. Twas the blasted Puritans who put a hole in my money bag, and tis they who accuse you now. Send for the girl. I'll have my wife watch over her. She'll come to no harm. But," and the man laughed hoarsely. "Twill still cost you your crown. Must make some profit."

Back out on the street, Ben signalled for Susanna and she came running.

"Where have you been? Tis getting dark and the street's no place . . ." she rattled on, but Ben blocked it off with a hand.

"Hush, we're going inside." And without waiting for an argument, one he knew she was preparing, he wheeled and sped into the backdoor of the inn.

Good smells brightened the kitchen—a trio of pots dangled over the fireplace, and Ben recognized the mixed scents of stewing veal, mutton, and beef. The tangy smell of a mincemeat pie rose from a stout wooden table. Dried red and green peppers hung from a thin wire strung across the room. He had grown up in just such a kitchen, and the chubby, grey-headed woman stirring the pots, cloaked in a long dress and stained apron, could have been his mother.

"Who are these people, Thomas?" Her cracked, aging voice broke across the room.

The man waved her off. "Just keep an eye on the girl. Come, lad." He headed to a door in the interior wall.

Ben followed along and the man stopped short of the passageway. He placed a hand on Ben's shoulder and shoved him roughly to the ground.

"This door opens behind the bar. Stay low and they'll never know you're there. Stand up and they'll see you in a flash."

Ben rubbed his aching knees and nodded.

As the door swung open, he heard light chatter and the clanking of tankards. Above him, all he could see was the thick rafters holding the ceiling aloft and a dim glow from the lit candles. He crawled across the threshold and hunkered against the bar. Thomas, the innkeeper, stood beside him, drying a clean tankard with a cloth.

"To your left," he mumbled down.

Ben scrambled to his left, almost to the end of the bar, and the voices became more distinct.

"Thanks for the tankard, John." It was Peter Carew.

"Yeah, tis appreciated." Arthur Digges' rasping voice was even clearer.

"My pleasure. A new day has dawned for all at the Globe, at least for all the apprentices. I doubt that we'll see Ben Jonson again. A murderer, who would have thought it. And Allan dead? Aye, there'll be a major re-shifting of roles. And," the boy preened, "there is another spot open for a new member."

"And you think you'll be asked?" Peter questioned.

"And why not? I've but a year to go on my apprenticeship and I'm the logical choice, if I wish it."

"What about the Arnold apprentice at the Curtain? They say Master Burbage has been there three times to watch him," Peter reminded Lambert.

"He is a good actor," Lambert grudgingly admitted.

"Better than you," Arthur said with a sneer in his voice.

"With Allan and now Ben gone from the stage, there will be ample chance to improve my craft," Lambert pointed out.

"Tis true," Peter's voice trembled a little. "But Ben was no bother and Allan was a likable sort. I'll miss him."

"At least till the next good role comes your way," Lambert quipped and all three laughed. "And, Peter, I doubt that you'll miss marks like that you sport on your cheek." A silence descended then which lasted several moments.

"Well, Master Lambert," Digges began. "Carew and I must take our leave of you. We've," and he harumpphed meaningfully, "things to do."

Chairs scraped and feet shuffled on the wooden floor.

"Maybe this time," Lambert said, "if you have any luck with the women, Peter, you won't get socked in the jaw for your trouble."

"You weren't there, John. You don't know the whole story."

"I know what you told me, that Allan clobbered you over the

Mayo wench. I've seen the black and blue color your face. Tis enough."

"Come on, Peter. Don't let Master Dandy ruffle your feathers. Let's go." Digges cajoled Carew.

"Have a good time!" Ben heard Lambert call after them.

He melted as far back against the hardwood of the bar as he could. The last thing he needed was to be seen hiding under a bar.

Only unfamiliar voices crept over his wooden sanctuary. Ben fidgeted. The innkeeper towered above him, pouring an occasional tankard of ale. His frustration grew, and grew. Finally, impatience breaking out like a rash, he reached up and tugged at the man's pants leg.

Thomas, the innkeeper, dropped a tankard, which landed next to Ben with a loud clunk. He bent to retrieve it, pausing at the bottom of his bend. "What is it?"

"What's the boy doing?" Ben hissed.

"You didn't pay me enough to do your spying for you."

"All right. Another crown then." It was the money Ben had saved for his sword, but this was important. They had to get at the truth of Allan's murder.

Thomas straightened and then knelt once more. "He's not doing anything. Just sitting there, drinking his ale."

"I'm going to leave," Ben whispered. Susanna must be driving the poor old woman crazy by now. And, he had to ask her about Carew's bruise. "Watch for me."

"Wait," came the reply. "A man just entered and is heading for your friend." The innkeeper spoke low and out of the corner of his mouth.

Ben swiveled back against the bar, bumping his head on the wood and stifling a cry of pain with his knuckle. Trying to ignore the ache in his head, he concentrated on listening. The raspy scrape of chair on floor sounded once again and Ben heard Lambert's voice.

"Master Armin, I'm pleased you made it."

So, Robert Armin was his "later appointment." Master

Shakespeare would find this most interesting. Ben focused in even closer on the pair.

"How goes it?"

"Fine, fine, Master. All is well. How have you done? Is it finished?"

"The matter is in hand, my young friend. There are still a few more to be dispatched, but the end is coming."

Ben swallowed hard.

"More? You are a devil, Master Armin. Soon there will be more dead bodies than the final scene of *Hamlet.*" A chuckle of envy sounded in Lambert's voice and Ben didn't miss it.

"Tis necessary. Tis necessary. I'm just pleased to be this near the finish. And, you, young sir, have been a great help. With Allan gone, you will receive more of the applause which you so richly deserve."

"Perhaps, perhaps. Though I don't deny that the idea is appealing, and due me, but I've just spoken to Deputy Sheriff Middlebury. He told me very clearly that I might soon find myself valuable to him. He said, and I quote, 'I have plans for you, my lad.'"

"Then, it seems, the theater might not be in your future."

"Master Middlebury can raise me higher than the Lord Chamberlain's Men might."

"Middlebury can be a slippery character, as we know," Armin warned.

The voices faded as the words struck Ben's ear. It was all true. Everything that Ben had feared and more. Master Armin was a member of the plot. But of course, Ben realized. Neither had anyone to vouch for their whereabouts backstage. And both were complicitous in Allan's murder. Along, it would seem, with Deputy Sheriff Middlebury. The pieces had all come together. Shakespeare. He had to get back to Shakespeare. Then, they could bring these murderers to justice.

He tugged again on the innkeeper's breeches. "I've heard enough. I'm leaving."

"Well, do it quietly," Thomas whispered.

Ben began a crawl towards the door, but something snagged his foot. Jerking his head back, he saw that the innkeeper had neatly slipped his own foot in to block Ben's exit.

"My two crowns, first," his host said out of the corner of his mouth.

"Urggh," muttered Ben. He twisted around and dug his last two coins out and laid them on the floor at the innkeeper's feet. "Pick them up yourself."

With a grin, the man released his foot and Ben scurried through the door.

"Isn't it time you told me what's going on?"

Ben had no more stood than Susanna was on him.

"Well." She crossed her arms and waited.

"No time for that, my girl. I've learned the truth. We've got to get to Master Shakespeare."

"What truth?"

"I said we have no time. Are you deaf? You're certainly not mute!" He grabbed her hand and pushed her out the backdoor, leaving the innkeeper's wife gaping.

"What did you find out?" She was persistent if nothing else.

Ben turned to her as they headed out of the alley and towards the street. "I discovered the minds behind Allan's death. Twas as I thought. John Lambert was a part of the plot. But so was Robert Armin, one of the other players. Shakespeare will be amazed at this new turn of events and we must get to him as quickly as possible. Afterwards, I can see that you get home, but right now it's more important for . . . Owwwh!"

"Ben Jonson!"

The young actor bounced off something and went spilling into the street. He sat up and shook his head to clear it. A familiar voice was calling him, but it wasn't Susanna's.

"Ben Jonson! Where have you been?"

He looked up and straight into the eyes of Robert Armin and John Lambert.

Seven

Twice and three times over his heart quickened. Susanna stood above him, speechless, and her eyes spun threads of fright that threatened to lock him in their embrace.

Ben scurried to his feet, slipping backwards and searching for words, but none would come. Armin started towards him. The sudden movement snapped Ben back to his senses.

He whirled towards Susanna and hooked her hand in his own paw. "Don't stand there. MOVE!!"

Ben dove through a gap in the crowded street, one that closed just as Lambert and Armin tried to follow. Glancing over his shoulder and beyond Susanna, who stayed fast on his heels, Ben saw Armin bowl over a housewife loaded with a cageful of chickens. Tangling his feet with those of the woman and a dozen chickens rambling around the lane, the angry-looking comedian landed face first in the cobblestoned street. Squawking, shrieking poultry filled the air.

"Stop, Ben!!" Lambert's voice broke above the clatter of a horse's hooves on the lane.

Ben dared not look back again. He put his small size to use, slipping between people and making spaces where there seemed to be none, and parting ways with Susanna in the rush. Footsteps and the cry of squawking chickens sounded on the cobblestones and

Ben knew that Lambert, at least, was still in pursuit. He checked behind him and sure enough, the lanky figure of his adversary was slicing as neatly through the crowd as he had.

"Ben! Come on!" Susanna stopped in the street ahead and urged him on. Ben pointed back towards Lambert, huffing and puffing up the lane. She glanced around swiftly and a gleam sparkled in her eyes. "Hurry!"

Ben dashed up beside her and she trotted across the street. A watchman sat on a street corner, head drooping into his hands.

"Oh, your Honor!" She fell on her knees as a very red nose, attached to a chubby-cheeked face, arose from its slouch. A look of alarm crossed his features.

"What is it, young mistress?"

"There's a man chasing me! Stop him!" She emphasized her words by grasping his hands.

The drunken watchman staggered to his feet and took up his stanchion. "I'll take care of the rogue, young missy."

He lurched forward as a wild-eyed John Lambert burst from the crowd, looking right and left for his quarry. "Halt, Sir, in the Queen's name!"

Lambert's eyes grew confused. "Who? Me?"

"Aye, you scoundrel. Stop chasing the lady!"

Ben and Susanna, with both silence and stealth, were slipping further and further away from the confrontation.

"Stop them, you old fool!" Lambert pointed at the retreating couple. "The man is wanted by the Sheriff."

The watchman snorted. "I saw no man, only a pretty young thing. And tis more likely you that the Sheriff is seeking. Stand, I say!"

Ben smiled from a distance as Lambert's frustration got the best of him. The apprentice feinted to the left and went to the right trying to rush past his adversary, but the watchman, apparently not as drunk as Ben thought, swept his cudgel low and clipped Lambert's legs from under him.

"Ooooff!" Lambert slammed against the cobblestones.

The watchman planted a foot square in the downed boy's chest and playfully clipped his chin with the end of the stick. "Move a hair, lad, and I'll put you to sleep."

Susanna grabbed Ben's arm and tugged at him. Ben followed, but kept an eye on Lambert and the frustration growing in his eyes. Finally, he turned his attention to the street ahead with a look of satisfaction.

"Your babbling almost put us in the cauldron for certain," Susanna chastised as they slowed to a fast walk, the bleating of John Lambert fading into the background.

"We're headed wrongly." Ben ignored her and glanced around. "Tis north we're pointed towards. Master Shakespeare awaits in Blackfriars to the south."

Susanna stopped in the middle of the lane and propped her hands on hips. "I'll not go anywhere until I catch my breath."

With a grunt of irritation, Ben pointed towards a cul-de-sac a half block up the street. Susanna nodded and started towards it, Ben following in her wake.

The sun was setting over Wales as Susanna half-collapsed onto a tired, old wooden bench set just inside the small alley. Ben plopped down beside her, his heartbeat trying to settle down to normal. Cool as it was, he felt hot and damp.

"What now?" she asked, her own chest heaving less violently.

"Should be easy. We'll just cut over a few blocks and give John Lambert and Master Armin a wide berth. Then, it's a simple matter of working back to Blackfriars as I said before."

"Aye. I've experienced your 'simple matters' before. Tis never as easy as you say."

"And tis not now!"

Ben and Susanna jerked their heads up. The strange voice sounded from the entrance to the alley, and there, blocking off the main street, were three men standing with feet spread. One carried a heavy cutlass, another a cat o' nine tails, and the last a club.

The rogue with the cutlass had a long, pink scar running down his cheek, across his throat, and disappearing into his blouse. He stepped forward and the others stood shoulder to shoulder behind him. A smile broke through the filth covering his face.

"Time someone took the starch out of you, lad. You've become a nuisance." The voice was almost jovial, but Ben knew that there was nothing playful in the man's intent. The way his cutlass point danced in the air told Ben that much.

Ben shot a look up the alley, but a blank wall met his eyes. One door opened onto the alley on the right side. He felt Susanna's hand grip his, tight, tighter than anyone ever had before. Night had almost fallen and beyond the alley entrance only the murky flush from a thousand candles in a thousand windows offered any light. From the darkness of the alley, the black forms of the men loomed huge against the glowing street.

"What do you want and who sent you?" Ben asked, stalling while he ransacked his brain for some way out.

The man with the cutlass grinned; Ben could just see the upturned corners of his mouth in the failing light. "Tis not for you to know. But comfort yourself. Tis someone who can pay the price to have you killed."

"And you'd kill me as well? Tis certain that you are not gentlemen." Susanna stood and faced their attackers.

Again, Cutlass smiled. "Tis certain," he agreed. "But methinks there might be more pleasure in delaying *your* death." His eyes roved over Susanna's maturing body. "Aye, the man dies first. The girl can provide us with some diversion. Our masters wouldn't deny us our needs, now, would they?" He glanced back to his companions who chuckled with him.

And Ben struck.

His head hit Cutlass just above the belt. The rogue went flying with a loud "OOOFFF!" Falling between his comrades, Cutlass grabbed to their clothes to hold himself up and succeeded only in pulling them down on top of him.

"Bastard!" The voice could have been Cutlass's or Club's, Ben didn't know.

Ben rolled to one side, slamming against a wall. "The door, Susanna! The door!"

Her eyes were glazed in confusion and she hesitated. Ben struggled to his feet almost at the same instant that Cutlass hoisted himself up. "The door, dammit!"

He willed her to go to the door in the side of the alley. It was their only hope. The rogue with the club had dropped it in the scuffle and Ben snatched the weapon from the ground. As if hearing his mental pleas, Susanna dashed for the door. Her hand closed around the knob and twisted. It opened, but she hesitated still, looking back towards Ben.

Cutlass regained his footing and slashed viciously downward, the blade reflecting the glow of candlelight. Ben threw the club up, just in time. The heavy metal sliced into the wood and stuck. He grabbed the other end of the club and wrestled with Cutlass. Twisting, he saw that Susanna was still waiting at the door.

"Go!!"

And she disappeared into the building.

With every ounce of power in his body, he pushed back on the club. Luck was with him. The shove denied Cutlass his balance and once again he went toppling backwards into his comrades, sending all of them sprawling on the ground.

Ben spun and sprinted to the door. The black yawning interior frightened him, but not as much as the cursing trio thrashing on the ground behind him. He held his breath and plunged.

"Ben!" Susanna's voice hissed somewhere up ahead.

He floundered through the room, unsure of his footing and his whereabouts. The building was apparently uninhabited and empty, at least no furniture bruised his shins as he stumbled along, and he concentrated on the swishing of Susanna's skirt in the blackness before him.

"Come, Ben." Her words floated eerily between the invisible walls.

He locked on to her voice and, bumping against an errant wall or two in his path, he felt his way through the house. A soft perfumed scent began tingling in his nose and he knew Susanna was close.

"Here," and her hand closed around his. "The front door is here."

A scuffle, maybe rats, maybe not, rippled through the rooms behind them. "Hurry," Ben urged.

The door swung open and a mix of candlelight and moonlight shafted into the room. A second later and they were on the street.

"Where to now?" Susanna breathed heavily.

Ben hesitated for just a minute. "North. We're too far out now and they're between us and Master Shakespeare. Time to find a rabbit's hole somewhere to harbor us. I think I know the place. At least I hope I do." The last words were mumbled. He squeezed Susanna's hand and headed north along the lane.

"Here they are!"

Cutlass and his companions rounded the corner at a run. Their detour had only bought them a little respite.

"I'll have no trouble sleeping this night," Susanna muttered as they bolted down the street.

Each pounding footfall on the cobblestones sent tremors up Ben's legs.

Twenty yards.

Thirty yards.

Fifty.

The race tore on, winding through the sparse crowd. Ben's heart pumped, pumped, pumped, almost breaking out of his chest. He stumbled, skidding to his knees. His britches tore, and so did the skin beneath. Pain ripped through him, but he struggled to his feet, Susanna pulling him up as best she could, and on they ran.

"Stop, you bastard!"

The scream broke through the night and Ben pushed his legs faster and faster.

Suddenly the sky lit up—Ben could see every brown and white, half-timbered shop and every greyish-brown stone in the pavement—and the rumble of thunder rolled across the city like a cannon's roar.

On he pushed, faster, harder, faster.

"Stop, damn your eyes!" blasted into his ears and he forced his tired legs on, and on, and on.

The rain came.

It came in sheets, ripping through the threads of his clothes and drenching his body. Susanna's hair no longer bounced; it hung limply, in clumps, sticking to her shoulders and Ben couldn't tell, in the brief glimpses he got of her face, whether there were tears mixed with the raindrops.

Glancing back over his shoulder, squinting his eyes against the rain, Ben tried to check on their pursuers. Their sprint had carried them beyond Bishopsgate, a half-mile or so south of Shoreditch. The rain had eased to a steady downpour. But even with that relief, he couldn't see or hear anything of Cutlass and his companions. It was as if they had disappeared.

The realization that they had outrun the trio hit Ben in the legs. They went numb. He slowed to a walk and then to a stop. "Wait, girl!" he cried.

Susanna turned and Ben winced at the fright etched into her face. He bent over and put his hands on knees, his lungs burning like a torch.

"The rogues?" she panted, coming to a halt.

"Can't see them. They . . . must . . . have . . . gotten lost . . . in the storm." The words emerged in rattled bursts. "Come on. We've got to . . . get out of the street." His breathing was returning to normal.

A look around revealed just a pair harmless travelers headed into the city. Few people were venturing north. Ben glanced up the road and, in the distance, saw the huddle of lights that he knew would be there. They were always there.

"Come, girl. There's only one place around here where we can seek solace and sanctuary."

"And where might that be?" Her tone of voice said everything about her confidence in Ben.

He grabbed her arm. "Just come along. We'll be safe in a few minutes." Starting off up the muddy lane, he muttered an epilogue to his prediction of security. "I hope."

❧ ❧ ❧ ❧

Shoreditch lay outside the city proper, beyond Bishopsgate and on the old Roman road in the north. Since it was such an ancient route, many inns had been built in the area. Several years earlier, James Burbage built his first theater in Shoreditch and it was soon joined by the Curtain. The puritans of London couldn't touch the players there and it became a refuge for the theater companies. And the parish had the reputation that went with the haunt of players.

Ben and Susanna trudged up to the patch of lights that was Shoreditch. Thatch-roofed buildings appeared alongside the road. Some sported fences in front of their doors, some didn't. At each, however, one or several young boys lounged around, often yelling good-natured insults to Ben and Susanna on the road as they drew into sight.

Ahead, Ben could see the big round shape of the Curtain to the right. No lights glowed in its portals. Plays weren't held at night, just in the afternoon, and never on the Sabbath. His eyes roved across the road from the theater until they lit on a monstrous, square, black thing looming up from the side of the road. A creaking sounded and Ben glanced up with a smile to see the sign—a leaping, bounding deer—dance in the wind.

"Ben! Is it truly you?" a young voice cried into the night.

Ben felt Susanna's fingers close around his arm and tighten. "Be at ease," he assured her. "We are safe here."

A small, lithe figure trotted from behind a fence and onto the road. "It *is* you, Ben!"

"Aye, brother, it is me."

At the word "brother," Susanna relaxed her grip. The features of a boy, ten or eleven, became clearer as small arms wrapped around Ben. "Tis too long since you last came, Ben. And who's the wench?"

Ben slapped his brother's cheek as Susanna suppressed a giggle. "Wench" sounded wrong on the youngster's tongue. "Stephen! Watch your mouth. This is Susanna Mayo of London. And this rascal, Susanna, is my brother, Stephen."

The boy looked a great deal like Ben, a little shallower in the chest and slimmer in the arms, but not a bad likeness at all. He was dressed in a brown vest and white shirt. His breeches came just below the knees.

"Where are the other hostlers?" Ben glanced around and saw no one else.

"Harold's sick and the Kennedy boy never showed up."

"So Father stuck you out here by yourself?"

The little boy shrugged in a "what can I say" gesture. "You know Father. The work must be done."

"This is your father's inn?" Susanna's voice did little to hide her surprise as she stared at the massive building.

"We can bed down two hundred a night if need be," Stephen said proudly.

"Aye," Ben grunted. "And Father would sell his soul to the Devil if he could get that many at one time. Tis not a fit night for such as you to be hostling by yourself. It wouldn't be the first time a hostler was knocked over the head for his charge's saddlebags." The hostler kept his station outside the inn and took immediate care of the arriving guest's horse, leading him around to the long row of stables behind the inn, and seeing to his feeding and bedding. Ben had spent many a day doing such chores and more than once he had found one of his fellows laid out with a bloodied skull and some tramp riding away on the horse.

"Father often reminds me that if you were still here I wouldn't have to be doing this," Stephen grinned at his older brother.

"Has Father forgotten that he agreed to my leaving?"

"Of course. The minute after it was done." The brothers laughed together.

The sucking of a horse's hooves in mud sounded down the lane and Stephen moved to the fence. "Go on to the kitchen. Mother's making supper. She'll be glad to see you."

Ben led Susanna into the yellowed light of the courtyard. Laughter and shouts spewed from the common room at the back of the yard. Above them rose the three stories of the structure, each level sporting a balcony, and Ben noted the absence of guests moving to their rooms.

"What's wrong?"

Ben realized that he was frowning. "It won't be a warm welcome, I'm afraid. Business doesn't seem to be booming."

❧ ❧ ❧ ❧

"God have mercy on us all!"

Ben's mother was a big woman, with a girth the size of St. Paul's, and a heart to match. She pulled her son in close and hugged him. Once a pretty, thin woman, the task of bearing four children (two died in infancy) and sampling her own wares in the kitchen had added pounds to Judith Jonson's presence. But she carried her weight well, and Ben's throat closed up as her familiar scent filled his nose.

"Sit, son, sit. Tis so long since I last saw you, and now you come, soaked and dirty, skulking in the door like a common rogue, and with this." She turned finally to Susanna. "Such a pretty slip of a girl. Sit too, child."

Ben, his legs feeling shaky, groped for a chair and slid into one. His mother bustled off to the far side of the kitchen as Susanna found a seat next to him.

"How is *dear* Master Shakespeare?"

He looked up to find his mother already putting a full plate of food in front of him.

"You mean the *murderer* William Shakespeare?"

Eight

he rasping voice shot through Ben like a rapier. He looked up to see his father, thin like him with a savage scowl across his face, stop just inside the door. Samuel Jonson carried a platter of dirty mugs and he set it carefully on the table.

"Father, you are so dramatic!" Ben's mother scolded.

"Is it not what the constable told us just an hour ago?" The irritation was thick in the older man's tone.

"But, Father, you know how rumors trickle up from Londontown. Certainly it's a misunderstanding. Tell him, Ben, tell him." She prodded Ben in the shoulder.

Ben's eyes had not wavered from his father. A friction, a web of harsh threads bound them together. "Tis true, Father. Master Shakespeare and I have been *accused* of murder." Samuel Jonson smiled a satisfied grin and Ben held his hand up. "But, the stuff of rumor is everchanging. Were it true, would I not already be in custody? Yet, here I sit, free as a bird, with no chains binding my soul, no shackles governing my steps. Reality and rumor are often brewed from different recipes."

"See, dear, the boy is all right. Just needs some dry clothes and a full belly." She pawed around on his dripping shirt. "Ah, tis fine clothes that Master Shakespeare has provided him. I told you he would do well by our son."

"I bought these myself," Ben said with a frown.

A scowl soured the older man's face. "Were it not for you, woman, the boy would be here helping with the inn. His apprenticeship ended almost a year ago. But I could only stomach so much 'William Shakespeare's a good man.' Would that he had never been born. And you," he turned back to Ben. "You have grown something of his silver tongue, but it will serve you for naught. For all your limber words, you cannot deny that the tides have turned against you and your friends. All of England knows by now of the Hawkins boy's death. My son, the consort of murderers." He sat down heavily in a chair.

Ben's knuckles whitened in anger, but he kept his tongue still.

Samuel Jonson gripped his knees and massaged them gently. "I've sat here across from that hellhole the Curtain for a score of years it seems. I haven't turned Puritan, but tis the truth that they speak about players and theaters." He stood, with more than a little effort, and walked slowly to a window in the back wall. Ben glanced towards the window and knew that his father was seeing the corner of the Curtain across the road. "How many days have I stood here and watched the heaving and shoving over there, just to get in and sit with the women. Aye, I've even crossed the road and seen them at their games. Playing footsie, tickling, toying, smiling, winking, taking them home when the play is ended for more play to begin.

"Oh, tis humorous to watch their sinfulness. And every sin conceivable in ancient Rome is committed across the road. Every wanton and his paramour, every man and his mistress, every John and his Joan, every knave and his queen are over there. Aye, over there, right across the lane from where I try my best to earn an honorable living, and that living gets poorer and poorer. No honorable man will stay in the shadow of that temple of Satan." His soliloquy was spoken quietly, but when he turned and faced Ben and Susanna, his eyes were fiery red. "And how am I paid for my honesty, my uprightness. I have nursed a viper in my bosom! My oldest child, the holder of this family's honor, lies with players!" He almost spit the last word out.

"Father, you exaggerate." Ben adopted a quiet tone, fighting with all his strength to control the anger building in him.

"Here you sit, the perfect proof of my words. Eight years ago, you were a fine lad, a son to be proud of. Now, after being perverted by these players, you show up on my doorstep, employed by a fugitive, and an accomplice to murder." Samuel Jonson looked at Susanna, noticing her for the first time. "And on top of that, you bring some bawdy-basket into your mother's kitchen. Have you no honor left, boy? Do you hold your family sacred no more?"

Ben leapt to his feet. "Had I no love for my family, I would strike you where you stand. You talk of me and my manners, but yet you make slanderous remarks against a girl whom you don't know, aye, one you've never seen before. I would say that her honor was just as intact as yours, but to do so might be to sully her name."

"I don't need you, Ben Jonson, to protect my honor!" Susanna was standing, a frightful glare reaching from her eyes. She turned to Ben's father and compressed her lips into a forced smile. "You, sir, could learn much from your son. I've seen more manners from the pigs in Cheapside than you've exhibited this night."

"OUT! I'll not have you in this house another moment!" Samuel Jonson's voice cracked in its bellowing.

Judith Jonson, who had shrunk into a corner, scurried out of the shadows. "No, Samuel. He is our son," she protested. "We cannot turn him out in the night."

"I can and I will," the older man replied. "He is no more the son I raised than is the commonest beggar in the lane. He made his choice when he stayed with Shakespeare after his apprenticeship. Leave now," he commanded Ben, "before I do something I'll surely regret."

"I wouldn't stay in this house another second." Ben's voice was soft, devoid of any emotion. His actor's skills served him well and hid the lump in his throat.

He took Susanna by the hand and, both still soaked to the skin, they went back out into the humid night.

❧ ❧ ❧ ❧

"What will you do now?"

Ben shrugged. He had just finished telling his brother, Stephen, about the debacle in the kitchen.

"I'll make my way back into London and try to get to Master Shakespeare."

"If father knew more of your trouble, he wouldn't toss you to the wolves. Tis poor business which has his humors unsettled."

"If father could keep his temper under control long enough, he would know about our trouble." Ben smiled at his brother. "But, you're right, his temper is not balanced. Aye, his anger is so out of balance that it topples his good sense."

"Tis nothing to make light of. I'm worried about you, Ben." Stephen hung his head and kicked at the mud.

Susanna lifted the boy's chin with a finger. "Your brother can handle any trouble that comes his way. Never worry about that." Her smile brought one just like it to Stephen's face.

Ben flushed a little and started back off for the lane. "Come, Susanna, we've a good distance to travel and it's well into the night." He looked at her and felt the urge to chuckle. His nerves had been strung so taut that it took little to ease the tension, and Susanna provided that little bit. Stringy, wet hair framed her face and sodden clothes clasped her body. Flecks of mud stuck to her cheeks looking for all the world like freckles. "We've got to get you cleaned up. Aye, your parents will have me horse-whipped if they should see you like this."

She raised her eyebrows at him as the smile widened on her face. "Would that you could see yourself in a looking-glass. I doubt that you would find it so funny."

"Tis certain that we have looked better. Let us get to my master. Where he is, there we'll be safe."

Wrinkles of concern wiped away her smile. She looked off towards the thousand pinpoints of light that were the candles of

London and shuddered. "Are they out there e'en yet, Ben, waiting for us?"

He took her by the arm and squeezed it gently. "Only time will tell, but we can't spend our days here. Master Shakespeare awaits us."

"Tis a bed which awaits you." The soft voice floated out of the darkness. Judith Jonson emerged from the shadows carrying a bundle of clothing. "Husband or no, my boy will face the world rested and in dry clothes or I'll lay no claim on the title 'mother.' Come, I've rooms ready for each of you and you can rest until your father has gone to bed."

"But, Mother . . ." Ben protested.

"I'll not hear another word. Stephen can fetch you in a couple of hours. You'll find things less fearsome with a pint of sleep under your belt." A no-nonsense look commanded Judith Jonson's eyes.

Ben hesitated for another second.

"I mean it, Ben Jonson. You'll do as I say."

He started to argue again, but his eyes crossed Susanna's face and her weariness touched him. "All right," he nodded. "Lead the way."

❧ ❧ ❧ ❧

"What hour is it?" Susanna's voice was hoarse, and Ben had heard her cough more than once.

He felt a tickle growing in his own throat. The rain had not returned but the cold night refused to leave even their new clothes dry, and the cloth hung on them heavy and wet. They had followed a zigzag path back into the city and were entering the area near Blackfriars.

"Tis hard to say. Midnight, not long after. Time to get you home." He reached down and felt, once more, the sword hanging from his belt. His mother had left it for him with the dry clothes. Ben grinned at the memory. "You may need it," she had said. She could be right, Ben thought.

"Nay. I cannot go home at this hour, and now that the chase is about to end, I want to watch the kill." Susanna shook her head as she spoke, the clumps of wet hair slapping her face with each shake.

A smile grew on Ben's face. Any other time, he would argue with her. But right at this moment, his energy was slipping away. Three hours sleep at his parents' inn had gotten him this far, but he didn't have much strength left. And to prolong telling Master Shakespeare his news was unacceptable. Robert Armin had warned that more would die, and if Ben wasted another single instant, it might cost lives. "Follow me, then."

The London of midnight was eerily quiet. Spots of light and laughter could be seen and heard, little pockets of life in a city asleep. Taverns in the city ran till the early morning hours and the constables would be busy at first light cleaning the drunks from their street-side beds.

"Click."

Ben froze. Something unnatural sounded; something out of place had echoed off the street.

"What is it?" Susanna asked.

Ben reached around and put a hand softly over her mouth. "I'm not sure," he whispered.

Her hand closed over his and slowly lowered it. Ben looked into her eyes and saw the shine of new fright. The fear of hours before returned quickly.

"Click."

The something sounded again.

"Let's keep walking. Down this way," he motioned down the lane. "If we can make it to the river, we can catch a ferry. He can't follow us there."

"Why not just run for it to Master Shakespeare?"

"The river's closer. He's trying to keep his distance, possibly even following us. It may be that he's looking for Master Shakespeare. I'll not help him in his quest."

Susanna nodded.

Ben licked his lips and glanced about. The cold air was damp and tasted foul on his tongue. He stepped off down the lane at a fast clip, just short of a trot. Susanna stayed close to him, the soft padding of her shoes comforting to his ears. But behind that padding lay an occasional, ominous clicking, like the sound of solid heels scurrying from place to place, staying just behind them.

Ben pricked up his ears and listened. Though the incessant noise of Londontown was diminished at night, it never really faded away completely. But in this section of town, a stone's throw from Blackfriars, nothing but the distant sound of ferrymen on the Thames disturbed the silence.

The ever-present mist drifted in from the water's surface and wrapped itself around the landscape. The street began its sloping descent to the river bank and he glanced about at the huge, black buildings looming over them, yawning cavernous doors opening to dark cave-like interiors. The clicking behind them was silent, but something in the silence sent a tingle down his spine. Time to move quickly, he thought.

"Come. Let's get to the ferry." He grabbed Susanna's hand and tugged her towards the river.

She didn't speak, just tightened her grip on his hand.

Ben headed at a fast walk on towards the river. Only the sound of their shoes on the packed earth echoed off the surrounding walls. For a moment. Then, other shoes thudded rhythmically off the lane. In the darkness. Behind them.

"Keep moving," he muttered. Half the fight, Ben knew, was holding it on your ground, where you knew the alleys and lanes, where you knew how to escape if the tide turned against you. If they could just make it to the river. Once at the river all would be well.

And just as the thought took hold, the river Thames was before him. But the jetty held an empty ferry and no ferryman. He stood, gaping at the murky river water lapping at the bank. Behind them, the rhythm of steps quickened on the lane. Ben turned to meet their pursuer.

He was masked and carried a heavy sword. A short, terse chuckle emerged from behind the mask and the man hefted his sword, slicing the air with it, silently inviting the pair to battle. Moving back and forth sideways, he kept a careful eye on his quarry.

Ben looked around. No Shakespeare, no help, no escape. Just a blundering female of no practical use at all. He turned back, with narrowing eyes, to his dancing enemy. His hand shot to the sword at his side and he unsheathed it in one smooth motion. With his free hand, he shoved Susanna away.

"Run for it."

"I'll not!"

"Don't argue with me, girl! Just do it!"

Hesitantly, Susanna faded into the shadows as Ben returned his attention to their opponent.

"What do you want with me?" Ben asked calmly, raising the point of his sword.

The masked man didn't answer; he began edging closer and closer to him, pushing him a step at a time to the lapping water. The point of his sword cut a smooth and rounded pattern in the air as he advanced. Gray eyes, sharp and glistening, followed Ben's every move.

Something hypnotic in the man's movements sent Ben inching backwards, giving ground before his attacker. Ben had never purposefully matched steel with a man before, though swordplay was a standard lesson for players, and a catch in his throat made him cough. He braced himself, held the sword high, and stood his ground, a curious, hard look holding his eyes and the eyes were riveted on the masked man.

"Methinks I've seen you before," Ben noted, his voice ringing loud and clear.

That same, coarse chuckle floated through the air and the masked man lunged.

Steel clanged against steel and Ben heard the sound echo off the far bank. The masked man thrust hard, but Ben sidestepped and parried the blow, a smile beginning to grow on his lips. It was easy to imagine himself on stage, but the sudden memory of Allan's stained doublet sent a chill through his stomach and wiped the grin away.

The young actor eyed his opponent with new caution and circled him. Suddenly, Ben slashed, the blade whirring through the air, but the masked man leapt back deftly, a look of respect growing in his eyes. Ben kept his adversary at a healthy distance with a constant thrusting of his sword, the memory of his sword lessons coming back more clearly with each passing minute. He had once seen cobras at a celebration; the mystic snakes had lain coiled, heads bobbing and weaving above their bodies, ready to strike at any moment. The mysterious fighter reminded him of those deadly reptiles.

Ben scanned the darkness about him, trying to see if Susanna had gotten away. His eyes widened as he thought he saw a familiar figure in the shadows. Suddenly, Ben's eyes grew even wider; his foot caught on the edge of a stone in the pavement and he tumbled to the ground. His heart raced and he felt the dampness of London closing in on him.

The masked man grinned fleetingly and moved in for the kill while Ben struggled to right himself. And he was quick, but not quick enough to stop his enemy. Standing over him, the masked man raised his sword to apply the coup de grace, his eyes cold and smiling.

Ben held his breath and awaited the blow.

But a queer look took hold over the gray eyes behind the mask. They slipped into blankness just as a thud sounded and the tinkle of broken glass littered the night. The attacker fell forward onto Ben's sword, upturned in a final effort to block the killing blow. He tumbled over sideways, impaled on the sharp blade.

Ben blew out a great breath and slumped back on the ground, his wrist throbbing from the wrenching of the sword. Susanna's slim figure appeared behind the stranger, the jagged remains of a bottle still nestled in her hand.

"I told you to run for it," Ben complained.

She grinned, a little shaken. "And if I had?"

"Can't leave the damned boat for a half a mo' without some evil coming round about." A muttering voice sounded from the darkness, gruff and, Ben thought, awfully familiar.

A lurching figure appeared from the shadows and its grizzled head stared down at the body. "Wasted my only bottle of port on him, you did. And for what, an ungrateful lout like you."

Ben reeled back under the man's breath. Susanna hadn't wasted the *whole* bottle of wine. That was for sure. Ben squinted for just a second and then it clicked. It was the old ferryman from the day of Allan's death, the man who couldn't take directions.

"Who in the hell's he?" the drunk asked, pointing down at the dead man.

Ben shrugged. "I'm not sure. Hold a moment and I'll slip off his mask."

Reaching down with his good hand, he pulled back the simple cloth cover.

"I'll be damned."

"Tis not unlikely," Susanna whispered. "But, who is he?"

"A man who would seem to have no part in this problem." Ben leaned back and a vague sort of moonlight crept across the dead man's face. It was the drunk who had bumped into Shakespeare at the tavern in Blackfriars. The same man they had seen twice that day. Was he just a drunk? Or had he been following them?

"Looks like a common rogue to me," the ferryman muttered, reaching down and jerking a bottle of ale from its hiding place. He yanked the cork out and sucked long and hard on the mouth. A hand, replete with dirty fingernails, wiped unceremoniously across his mouth. "Good riddance to him, I say, good riddance."

"Ben, you should go for the constable," Susanna decided after a moment's silence.

"Ye Gods! Are you mad, woman?" The old man looked at her incredulously. "Tis madness for certain." He kept shaking his head.

"But a man has been killed," she argued.

"Says who, young missy? I've not seen anything. Have you, sir?" The ferryman turned to Ben.

Ben's stomach was churning. An icy sweat masked his face. "What?"

"Grab his feet," the old man ordered.

Ben stooped over and wrapped his hands around the corpse's ankles. The ferryman did likewise at his wrists. With the old man leading, they picked up the body, heavy as ten sacks of potatoes, and tossed it onto the ferry.

"Leave it to me, girl," the ferryman continued, brushing his hands off. "I'll see that no one finds this highwayman for many a day. You two hightail it somewhere else. On with you!"

"I'll not forget this," Ben said.

"Then don't," his benefactor grumped. "But on with you so an old man can get to work."

Ben nodded a quick nod and grabbed Susanna's elbow, turning her away from the river and back into the darkness that was London. He half-expected another argument, but she followed without a sound.

❧ ❧ ❧ ❧

"In the name of God, boy! What has happened to you? And why is this girl with you still? Answer, boy! Answer!" A worried and angry William Shakespeare stood over the pair in big Ben Jonson's house. Young Ben had rid himself of his shock after a few moments at the ferry landing and he directed Susanna to his namesake's house, both running on some unnamed, unknown strength.

"Much has happened, Master," he answered with a snap, his nerves raw and jangling. Shakespeare's words grated on him.

"Will Shakespeare! Bring them to the table! Now!" Anne Jonson's tone left nothing to the imagination and Shakespeare held his tongue while she placed steaming bowls of soup before them.

"Now," he said finally. "Kindly explain to me why you disobeyed my orders. And I expect a sensible answer."

"Remember this, William Shakespeare, I am your apprentice no longer; nor am I bound to follow your every order!" Anger gripped Ben and reddened his ears.

Anne Jonson froze in her steps; Susanna stopped the spoon headed to her mouth; and William Shakespeare stared intently at his former apprentice.

A long second passed as color sprang into Shakespeare's cheeks. But, as he and Ben matched each other stare for stare, the color receded.

"No, Ben Jonson," Shakespeare spoke softly and gently. "You are not my apprentice any longer. But you are my friend."

The anger faded across Ben's face. "Yes, . . . well, . . ." he said, uncomfortably. "We had hoped to be back sooner."

"Yes," Shakespeare said politely, and expectantly.

"Our journey was productive." Ben wiped the remaining film of soup from his lips and smiled a tired, but triumphant smile. "We have discovered the murderer, Master."

"Is that so? Tell me, tell me."

A hint of sarcasm seemed to lie in Shakespeare's words, Ben thought. But he plunged in anyway. "We watched as the funeral procession ended and saw Lambert in deep conversation with Walter Hawkins."

"So?"

"So, Master Hawkins slipped a note in Lambert's pocket."

"Is this all you have to say?"

"Hardly."

"Well, my lad, tell it all and quit dragging it out! I've been out of my wits worrying about you." Newly creased lines scored the playwright's forehead, the gentleness of the past moment drifting away.

A wave of guilt without anger washed over Ben, for just a second. He described how they had eavesdropped on Lambert, Carew, and Digges, and how he and Susanna had followed them to the Crosskeys Inn.

"Did they not see you?"

Ben shook his head. "I thought once they did, but Digges and

Lambert were arguing and didn't notice me. We were very careful."

"Go ahead."

"I managed to hide behind the bar and listen to their conversation. . . ."

"At a price, I imagine. Thomas does nothing for free."

"If you want the story," Ben began, the irritation heavy in his voice, "then let me finish!"

Susanna, sitting next to him, chuckled until Ben elbowed her.

"Now," he continued, Shakespeare suppressing a grin of his own. "I listened to the three talk, but it was most boring to be quite honest with you. Though I did find out why Allan beat Peter Carew."

"And why was that?"

"Because he had eyes for Mistress Mayo here."

"Allan Hawkins never touched Peter Carew!"

Nine

usanna Mayo's tone had never been more firm.

Ben gaped at the stubborn look on Susanna's face. Shakespeare looked at her quizzically.

"I'm sure you're mistaken, young Mistress. Ben and I both saw the mark."

"And I'm equally sure I'm not. Certainly, Peter liked me and he knew of my liaison with Allan. Peter and I were children together. He mooned around some, but Allan simply ran him off. He had no jealousy over Peter. My likes have never run to his sort. Allan thought the whole thing humorous, and indeed, if the truth be known, he liked Peter for all his whining. If Peter Carew bears a mark, it did not come from Allan Hawkins."

"And you are certain of this," Shakespeare pressed.

"Aye, as certain as I am that you're William Shakespeare."

"Why didn't you tell us before?" Ben was frowning heavily.

She shrugged. "It didn't seem important."

"Twas merely an unanswered question." Shakespeare stopped the brewing fight. "But tis worth remarking on. Let's go forward."

"Tis an odd thing," Ben mumbled. "Well, Digges and Carew left and Lambert was alone for a time. Then he was joined by another, his conspirator companion in this enterprise. They spoke boldly of the death of Allan and spoke of more to come. Aye, Lambert and this fiend compared it to the last scene of *Hamlet.* I would never have guessed it, but it fits in with what we already knew."

"What fits in?"

"Lambert's companion in murder."

"Blast your hide, man! Who was it!" Shakespeare's gentle countenance turned a furious red. "You would try a dead man's patience."

"Master Robert Armin." Even in his exhaustion, Ben allowed himself a smile of self-satisfaction. "Armin and John Lambert conspired to take Allan's life. Why, Armin even thanked Lambert for his part in the affair."

"Did they admit to it directly?"

"Well, no, not in so many words, but their intent was more than obvious."

"But how does Walter Hawkins fit into this plot."

Ben knitted his eyebrows in concentration. "Obviously, when Allan proved unwilling to wound one of us, he had to be eliminated. And what better way then to have him killed on stage, thus *proving* our decadent ways and getting rid of an obstacle. Lambert has always been drawn by position and money. He would have been easy to convince on this enterprise. Hawkins, who you must remember was not Allan's true father, must have gone straight to Lambert for help. He gave it, most bloodily. Aye, it may even have been money that Middlebury slipped into Lambert's pocket on the street."

"And what of Master Armin?"

"Why, he must be in some financial need, or perhaps he's a secret Puritan. He certainly chased us with enough vengeance."

"Chased you? Marry, you haven't told me of this."

Ben explained about the encounter with Armin and Lambert and then the subsequent confrontation with Cutlass and company. As he spoke, his big namesake came down the stairs, rubbing his tousled red hair, and took a seat at the table. A thoughtful look grew over Shakespeare's face.

"How much time elapsed between the two encounters?"

"Not more than five minutes. Armin and Lambert must have moved quickly to hire those ruffians. Or perhaps they had them round about."

"Twas very convenient," Shakespeare agreed. He tugged at his gold earring and stayed silent for a moment. "Surely there is some truth in what you say. That I would not deny. But methinks there are other avenues which will prove more profitable. Aye, the whole affair is becoming clearer by the second."

"There is more. I killed a man."

Shakespeare's eyes narrowed. "What?"

Ben described the fight at the river with the masked man.

"Did you unmask him?" Shakespeare queried.

"Aye. Do you remember the drunkard that we saw twice that day at the tavern here in Blackfriars?"

"Surely."

"Twas him."

"Remarkable. What of his body?"

"That senile old ferryman took it out on the river and 'lost' it for us."

"Astounding."

"You certainly have an interesting life, Will," Big Ben Jonson said. "Anne sent me down to convince you to take your circus elsewhere. She's afraid I'll wind up in jail once more."

"And what did you tell her?"

"That tis such as you that keeps my days from being a bore. Besides, who else in all London could I spar with as well as you?"

"You flatter me. But, now that young Ben Jonson has returned to the fold, perhaps we can bring this affair to a conclusion." Shakespeare stared sternly at Ben, while the boy's famous namesake grinned at him.

"He has spirit, Will," Big Ben Jonson said. "Give him credit for that at least. It took a great heart to lay into those rogues as he did. That is, if he didn't embroider it some. He was your apprentice after all."

"Nay," Susanna exclaimed. "He tells every bit the truth. Not a braver heart lives."

Shakespeare and his friend Jonson smirked at each other. "Then let no more doubts be cast on his spirit," Jonson said.

"Aye," Shakespeare grumbled after a moment. "Spirit he has aplenty. And, were it older days, even less hide he'd have when I got through with him. But, I must admit that you have provided some much needed pieces to this puzzle, Ben. You've proven yourself quite capable."

"Then, you agree, Master, that John Lambert and Robert Armin are the men we seek." The certainty was strong in Ben's voice.

Shakespeare grinned. "I don't think that we are ready to draw that conclusion. Tis one more act to be played, and that the telling one."

"I think I've had my final scene," Ben said, his weary head drooping towards the tabletop.

"Screw up your courage, my lad."

"Tis not my courage which needs screwing up, but my eyelids. Some witch has bedeviled them."

"What of me?" The weariness was heavy in Susanna's eyelids as well.

Shakespeare stroked his earring. "You were distraught after Allan's funeral," he began. "You went walking and were accosted by two men. A constable assisted you, but so upset were you that you lost your senses and took on a trance. Ben's wife, Anne, was buying chickens and brought you to her house. Twill only be at daylight that you have your wits about you and can tell her where you live."

"Anne won't like you for this," Ben Jonson warned.

"Your wife doesn't like me that much anyway. Tis little to put to chance." Shakespeare laughed. He turned to Susanna. "At first light, Master Jonson will have Anne take you home and explain everything. For now, I'm sure they will give you a place to—"

"No! I'll not be shunted off to home. I'll see this affair to its end."

"She has been much abused, Will," the red-headed giant reminded him.

"True." He paused for a few minutes and studied the girl. "Then, rest easy, Mistress Mayo. When the final act is played, I'll see to it that you have a prime seat."

Anne Jonson, who had just walked in, took Susanna by the arm and led her up the stairs.

"What about a bed for me?" Ben croaked.

"Tell me, Ben," and Shakespeare ignored the young actor's plea, turning to the red-headed giant, "of a lawyer who I might see eye to eye with."

"One to help you out of your situation?"

"Aye, precisely."

"There is a young man, one I've known for some time. I'll send for him and have him meet us here."

"Splendid. While we wait, you can tell me once more how I lack art."

"Art!" Ben Jonson cried. "You lack the Three Unities, you lack structure and form. You are witty beyond belief and comprehension, but. . . ."

Young Ben found a smile growing on his face as their host berated his master, and, despite the hardness of the table planks against his cheek, sleep finally came.

❧ ❧ ❧ ❧

The sounds of voices broke his slumber. Ben found himself still smiling and stopped as he realized that the face of Susanna Mayo floated lazily in his mind's eye. He shook his head to clear it and then opened his still heavy lids to see Shakespeare, Jonson, and a third man, young, not much older than himself, and bookish, lifting tankards and joined in deep conversation. Ben frowned. Something about this stranger was familiar.

"I've read *The Rape of Lucrece,*" the newcomer was saying. "I found it sentimental at best. Too traditional. My own poetry, though not published," and he mockingly bowed towards Shakespeare, "reflects our changing world."

Ben Jonson threw back his enormous red head and laughed. "Your poetry, John Donne, deals more with your efforts to bed some hapless maid than with some new world view."

Ben's eyes narrowed. So, this was the lawyer they had seen with Walter Hawkins at the funeral. He wondered why Shakespeare had summonsed him.

"Perhaps," Shakespeare grinned, "poetry is the bed in which he hopes to sow his seeds of knowledge."

Young Ben raised his head and cast a sorrowful look at his master. "God save us," he groaned, "from your wit."

"Amen!" cried the other Ben Jonson. "Will, why do you adhere so strictly to the classics in your poetry and then ride far afield in your plays? Tis incomprehensible."

"No. Tis a fact. I find the classic forms quite appealing for verse, but to imagine setting a play within a single day, or in a single place with only a single action. Bah! You are one of the few, Ben Jonson, who can produce respectable work within such constraints."

"But what you do has no merit."

"Tell that to the groundlings who pay their pence to watch my meritless plays."

"You are impossible!" Big Ben Jonson's face turned as red as his hair, but Donne reached over and patted his hand.

"Be at ease, my friend," Donne began. "There is something to what Master Shakespeare says. Our world's views on everything from art to the heavens ride restlessly on the waves of a troubled sea."

"Bah! And you, John Donne, your best work is behind you. Tis true that I consider you first among poets for *some* of your works, but others are pure and simple blasphemy."

Donne's face twisted in chagrin. "You do not understand me."

"You do not make yourself understood," countered Jonson.

"New philosophies are often unsettling and confusing," agreed Shakespeare, jumping into the fray. "And people twist things to suit themselves. Look at the Puritans." He reached across the table and yanked up a broadside—poster—laying there. "I'll not ask why you have this upon your table, Ben Jonson, but it is full of fantasy. Listen to what they say of us. 'They are a special cause of corrupting their youth, containing nothing but unchaste matters, lascivious devices, shifts of cozenage, and other lewd and ungodly practices, being so as that they impress the very quality and corruption of manners which they represent, contrary to the rules and art prescribed for the making of comedies even among the heathen, who used them seldom and at certain set times, and not all the year long as our manner is.'"

Shakespeare paused and took a breath. "Sounds like something you've written, Ben."

The giant red-head glared at the playwright.

"But," Shakespeare continued. "They do know much about comedy. Look at my friend Geoffrey Middlebury. He cuts a most comic figure. And tis he who has caused me to send for you, John Donne."

Donne smiled hesitantly. "I was honored to be called by the great Shakespeare."

"You thought your purse might profit from coming," grunted Jonson.

"Seems to me that such a downright scholar," young Ben inserted, "would know better than to consort with the likes of Master Middlebury and Master Hawkins. I do not trust him."

Donne recoiled from the young actor, shock and amazement spreading across his face. "You are an unappreciative upstart."

Shakespeare cocked an eye and stroked his beard. "Twas you, Master Donne, who was with Hawkins and Middlebury at the funeral yesterday. Aye, he may be impertinent, but he has the truth about him."

Donne stood quickly, sharply. "I did not come here to be accused and misunderstood." He straightened his blouse. "I just recently got out of prison, a misfortune that many of us have not avoided. The law is what I was trained for, so I've been trying to support myself and my wife, Anne, by doing legal work. Walter

Hawkins sent for me to draw up some bills of sale and deeds. When his son died, it seemed a natural thing to attend the funeral."

"And certainly didn't hurt your standing with the wealthy Master Hawkins," replied big Ben Jonson. Donne's frown deepened, and Jonson continued. "Just a comment, John."

"Sit, Master Donne. You weren't brought here to have accusations made against your character." Shakespeare pointed towards the chair.

"Seems a more profitable purpose than all this sitting around and talking about poetry and the changing world and who Master Donne is making the beast with." Young Ben yawned and stretched, the sleep finally easing out of his eyes.

"Quiet," Shakespeare began. "John Donne is no more the enemy than you are. And we have need of his legal skills now. That is, if he is half as sharp-minded as your larger half here says."

"I'm not sure I like your tone, but. . . ." Donne hesitated.

"But he needs the money," Jonson finished for him. The lawyer nodded and sat back down.

"One question, Master Donne," Shakespeare began. "Which is greater: An arrest order from the London Council or a command from the Queen?"

"Why, the Queen's command, of course."

"Can nothing else overrule?"

"I suppose that an order from Parliament might, but tis a question of jurisdiction and authority in local matters."

"Then there is no question of the Queen's primacy, especially if someone is willing to pay to obscure her primacy? Would fifty crowns change your mind?"

"No, not at all. No such bribe can change the hierarchy of the law. The Queen's word *is* law. Were she a weaker monarch, perhaps, but this one is far from weak. And I am not one to question the law, merely abide by it. I am disappointed by your attempt at bribery. I thought better of the great William Shakespeare."

A smile broke across Shakespeare's face and he rubbed his hands together. "Excellent. I have no intention of bribing you, Master Donne. Rather, I have a message for you to take back to your client, Walter Hawkins, and his companion, Deputy Sheriff Middlebury."

Both Ben Jonsons frowned.

"Tell them that you have lately been in the company of the infamous Ben Jonson, friend of the murderer William Shakespeare. Tell them that Jonson told you that the Globe company has been commanded to present a special performance of *Twelfth Night* one day hence at the Globe, and that rumor is about that Shakespeare will be present. Tell them that they'll never have a better opportunity to catch him. You tell them that."

Concern masked Donne's face. "I have never questioned you about the charges which have been levied, Master Shakespeare. I assumed that it was just another Puritan trick, but I beg you, don't make me run afoul of the law once more. If they will send me to prison for marrying the woman I love, they'll not hesitate to imprison me for conspiring with you. I didn't enjoy my stay in the Marshalsea. And I've been out but a fortnight."

"Deliver your message well, be present at the performance, stand ready to offer the same opinion on the Queen's primacy, and you will be better off than ever before. Trust me."

"Sir." Donne shook his head. "You woo me like a wanton woman. Tis glad, I am, that I haven't yet run afoul of you. But why the questions of the Queen's authority? Tis a simple enough issue."

"Aye, but I needed to know how your principles stood in relation to your purse."

"Then, it was a test of my nature."

William Shakespeare nodded a mock bow. "I am but a simple man, Master John Donne, not gifted with your insight into the world around us. Such tricks are sometimes necessary."

"What are you up to? And how will this bring Allan's murderer to the gallows?" His companion was not impressed with Shakespeare's modesty. Little Ben's namesake, the big bluff giant, leaned forward too, anxious to hear the answer.

The playwright remained silent for a few seconds, staring at the rugged beams in the ceiling. His head slowly leveled and his eyes met Ben's. "The play's the thing, my lad. The play's the thing."

Ten

reat God, Will Shakespeare! Where have you been? All of England searches for you!" Richard Burbage half-walked, half-ran across the stage as Shakespeare and Ben entered one of the side doors.

Madness reigned at the Globe. Apprentices and actors scurried back and forth with racks of costumes and stage properties. Cuthbert Burbage, less the performer and more the manager than his brother, directed traffic amidst the pandemonium. It seemed to Ben more a scene of destruction than impending performance.

"Hello, Richard. Tis a pleasure to be back."

"'Tis a pleasure to be back.' Is that all you have to say? Accused of murder, the High Sheriff demanding that you surrender, and a performance demanded by the Queen! Aye, and a queer demand at that."

"Demanded by the Queen? The High Sheriff? This is all disjointed. Richard, I don't understand. Speak slowly, Master Burbage. You are too overwrought. And why is everything being moved?"

"You don't know?"

Shakespeare tugged his earring and smiled. Ben knew his master was gaining great enjoyment from playing the innocent with Burbage. "Know what? Richard, please be plain. I haven't time for teasing. Great charges have been made against me." His solemn tone was almost frighteningly real.

Burbage shook his head. "We have been commanded to present a special performance of *Twelfth Night* this evening. A messenger from the Master of the Revels arrived within the hour. And your presence was particularly commanded." The actor stroked his pointed beard feverishly. "No explanations! No chance for rehearsals! The play is to be performed here and the Queen's not even in town. I understand little of this. Tis some evil in the air, Will. I doubt it not. Aye, I've not even had time for any special rehearsals with the ladies, if you catch my drift. But, all that tis beside the point. What of you? And why did Robert Armin and young Lambert have to chase Ben through the streets?"

"I am well, Richard. And as Ben, here, can vouch, I am not a murderer. Tis a fantasy of Master Middlebury that would make me one. And, to answer your final question, why did Robert and John *want* to chase Ben?"

"Well," stuttered Burbage. "The charges, Will, the charge of murder. Surely you cannot fault them for wanting to talk to Ben."

"The charges are unfounded, Richard. Totally unfounded."

"I warned you, Will. I warned you to let the constable take charge of this matter." Burbage shook a finger at Shakespeare as a worker whirled by with a rack of costumes, tipping Burbage off his balance and sending him reeling.

"Here, now, Richard." Shakespeare let Burbage steady himself on his arm. "All is well. Or will be well. There may be some mischief performed e'en yet. But we shall be ready for it. What of Henry?"

Burbage's head drooped. "Not good. I visited him yesterday. He doesn't wear the prison well. But, his spirits are not as bad as they could be. He has great faith in you. I'm not convinced that faith is well-placed."

"You wrong me, sir. Have I not caused more commotion than Clarence Parkes could ever have created?"

"Aye, and gotten yourself accused of murder at the same time. Tis well that you don't search out murderers more often. They'd charge you with treason."

Shakespeare smiled. "Time will tell, my old friend. Let us settle affairs with the play first. Have all arrangements been made?"

"All but the parts. Cuthbert must know who to give the players' sides to. We've not performed *Twelfth Night* since Allan's death. Aye, we've not performed aught but one play. The axe was bound to fall any day and the Globe closed, so we cancelled the schedule. We were preparing for *Richard III.* Now, this. A command performance with no notice."

"We'll have time to assign parts before long. Most will remain the same, anyway. Have you got things organized?"

Burbage looked at him incredulously. "Are you serious, man? Look about you! Does it not seem organized?"

Ben suppressed a chuckle as Shakespeare coughed into his hand. "I'll go find Cuthbert and lend a hand. Ben, you see what you can do to help. Richard," and Shakespeare turned back to his friend, "have no worries. Twill all be over in a matter of hours." He spun on his heel and started off across the theater grounds.

"Wait! Will Shakespeare! Don't do me like this! Tis more you must tell me!"

And Ben laughed out loud as Burbage, arms flailing, trailed Shakespeare through the building.

❧ ❧ ❧ ❧

Royal performances were major events in the life of a players' company. Ben had acted before Queen Elizabeth on several occasions during his time. A company's stature was judged by the number of its invitations to perform at court. And Ben knew that his master's plays were no small reason for the privileged status their company enjoyed.

But an extra excitement ran through the apprentices, players, and hired men this time. No one could remember such a summons from the Office of the Revels, the agency in charge of arranging entertainment for the sovereign.

Rumors and half-truths reached Ben's ears all morning.

"It's a trap to capture Master Shakespeare."

"The Queen is going to become our patron."

"We are all to be condemned and executed."

"The Queen is coming back to town to name James as her successor and we're to be part of the celebration."

"The Queen is dying and the doctor hopes our performance will enliven her."

It didn't matter that there was no basis to any of the rumors.

Ben stayed with Lambert, Carew, Digges, and Harrison all morning. He didn't understand what his master's plan might be, but he was sure that Lambert would turn out to be the villain. Everything pointed in that direction.

"Ben!"

The young actor jumped. Digges, Lambert, and Harrison were staring at him.

"Toss me your knife," Digges asked. He was holding a rope wrapped around a rolled up canvas. Ben complied and Digges, knife in hand, quickly tied it off and cut the excess.

"Lost in dreams of glory, Master Jonson?" Harrison chided.

Ben blushed. "Sorry."

"Tis all right. Tis been an unsettling day for certain," Harrison consoled.

"Don't worry, Ben," Lambert grunted. "Just send the Queen word that you prefer to play another day and I'm sure she'll change her mind."

"I've no interest in your insults, John." Ben was indeed in no mood for sparring with Lambert.

"Aye, maybe, but you certainly did your best to make a fool of me in the lane yesterday." Lambert rubbed a slight bruise on his chin. "And why Master Burbage doesn't turn you in to the constable is—"

"Something," Harrison interrupted, "that is none of your business."

"John's just afraid they'll make him play Maria," Digges quipped, breaking the tension. "Rather Peter here should play the role. He has the breasts for it."

"Shut up, Arthur!" Ben snapped. "There's no time for such tomfoolery."

"Aye, he's right. More work to be done than we can see." Harrison moved in to separate the boys.

"Tis true, Master Harrison," Ben sighed. "Tis true."

❧ ❧ ❧ ❧

"Maria! Please Master Shakespeare. Have someone else do this role." Peter Carew was waving his "side," his list of Maria's lines.

They had gathered at centerstage at the Globe for the assigning of parts. Only a few parts had to be shifted. Allan Hawkins's death necessitated at least one change, Henry Condell's arrest prompted another, and the actor who played Sir Toby Belch had gone to his father's funeral in St. Albans.

Robert Armin had protested just as fiercely at Shakespeare's presence as John Lambert had at Ben's. "Tis just asking for trouble," Armin had said. "Nothing against you, Will."

"No offense taken, Robert."

"I don't ask to know your private affairs, Will, but enough is enough. Twill take all our efforts to keep our doors open as it is. And this performance! The Queen commanded it, but she's not even in town. It could be a test of us. Who knows who will sit in the galleries this noon. We don't need a pair of fugitives in our house."

"This is all nonsense," Richard Burbage had replied. "The Master of the Revels commanded Will's presence. And Will shall be here."

And that had settled that.

"Ben." Shakespeare ignored Carew's pleadings. "You shall have the role of Viola."

He nodded. Out of the corner of his eye, he saw a frown grow on John Lambert's face.

"Master Lambert, are you up to Sir Andrew Aguecheek?"

The grimace on Lambert's face was replaced by a smile. "Of course." The Aguecheek role was one played by Henry Condell. To be assigned an adult role was a signal honor. He snatched the list of lines and wandered to the edge of the stage.

"Arthur, can you handle Sir Toby Belch?"

The wild-haired apprentice cocked an eyebrow. Two adult roles played by apprentices—an unusual performance at the least. "The lines are no problem, Master."

"What then?"

He patted his belly. "I'm too skinny."

Cuthbert Burbage laid an unusually kind hand on the boy's shoulder. "Some padding will take care of that."

"Master Shakespeare," Peter Carew moaned. "Please give somebody else Maria's role."

"There is no one else."

"Please!"

"No. It is settled."

"Back to work, lads," Cuthbert Burbage ordered. "We've a play to perform."

❧ ❧ ❧ ❧

Ben peeked out from behind the curtain. His breathing came in labored bursts. Around him, Cuthbert and one of the hired men moved the last few things into place. All had to be ready in moments. Harrison, the carpenter, was fiddling with the props. A great crowd was present in the galleries and the ground. Cuthbert had just barely the time to send some boys out with billboards to plaster up, announcing the performance.

"Quite a sight."

Ben looked around. Shakespeare and Susanna had appeared over his shoulder. "You made it," he said to Susanna.

"Aye. Master Shakespeare let me slip in. And, he's right. Tis quite a sight."

"Aye. No matter how many times we perform, I always like to watch the crowd gather."

"Master Shakespeare?" Susanna asked.

"Yes, Mistress Mayo."

"I know that all this has something to do with Allan's death, but I can't see how Lambert will be brought to heel by this performance."

Shakespeare stroked his beard for a moment and didn't speak. His eyes were locked onto something in the crowd. "I'm betting on man's greed and his obsessive nature."

"And if you lose?"

"I won't. Where's your dagger, Ben? You may need it before the night's over."

"Gave it to Digges when we were packing for the trip. I'll get it back."

Shakespeare raised an eyebrow. "A man's dagger should never be far away from him. Could get you killed in a tavern some night." The playwright spun and disappeared into the backstage bustle, taking Susanna with him.

Cuthbert hurried past Ben, yanked on the lanyard, and the curtain opened. The Prologue, an actor who gave the audience an introduction to the play, stood at dead center stage. He opened his mouth to speak.

"Hold!" A voice rang out across the hall.

All murmurs fell silent and Ben, still peeking out from backstage, searched for, and found, the owner of the voice. Geoffrey Middlebury.

"What pure, brazen audacity," Shakespeare whispered in Ben's ear. "The man lacks not for stupidity."

Middlebury strode towards the stage. Two club-toting constables, one the chubby, red-headed Clarence Parkes, hurried alongside him.

Cuthbert Burbage walked out onto the stage and looked down at the Deputy. "Who are you and what right do you have to stop this play?" His shaggy hair reminded Ben of a lion's mane, and

Ben knew, too, that Cuthbert was well aware of who Middlebury was.

"I am Geoffrey Middlebury, Deputy Sheriff of London."

Cuthbert gave him a "so what?" look. "You answered only half my question."

"William Shakespeare is in this building." Middlebury spit the name out.

Ben tensed. He felt Shakespeare's hand on his shoulder squeeze just a fraction harder than usual, and then Shakespeare walked past Ben and onto the stage proper.

"That man is wanted for murder. He must be arrested before he can cause more harm. Tis for the public's safety." Middlebury's words were spoken with firmness, confidence, and the audience reacted with an audible gasp.

The constables, Clarence Parkes waddling ceremoniously, started for the stage with Middlebury, and Ben clenched and unclenched his fists tightly. As they drew closer, Cuthbert Burbage motioned some of the other players together and they formed a barrier around Shakespeare. More than one had his hand on his sword.

Middlebury scowled at the makeshift bodyguard. He tried to push through the ridiculously padded Arthur Digges, but the boy gave no ground and the Deputy fell back.

A man, one who looked familiar to Ben, leapt down from the gallery, pushed past the groundlings, and approached the stage.

"Stop," the young man cried. He was fashionably dressed in a ruffled blouse and tight hose. "We'll not interrupt the entertainment for this matter. The play will continue."

A rumble of disapproval rolled through the Globe, adding strength to Middlebury's cause. "Who, sir, are you?" he asked with a sneer.

"I am Henry Wriothesly, the Earl of Southampton."

Middlebury paled. He swallowed hard and began again, in a softer tone. "My Lord, I beg your pardon, but it is the law."

"Perhaps, and perhaps not," Southampton answered. As the young earl spoke, two other men moved next to Middlebury.

"Your Lordship," one said, and Ben sighed in relief. It was John Donne. "If it please your Grace."

"You are . . . ?"

"John Donne, a lawyer."

"Continue."

"I have just consulted with the Master of Revels here," and he indicated the other man, "and we concur that Master William Shakespeare is protected by Parliamentary law in this matter. The law cites that players who have been commanded to perform by the Queen are secure from arrest while traveling to the site of the entertainment, while there, and until they arrive back at their place of origin." The man next to Donne nodded his agreement. "Since the Queen commanded this performance, this man, and his fellows, are protected by law from arrest."

"It is decided," concluded Southampton. "My friends," and he waved toward a group of equally well-dressed courtiers in the gallery, "and I are expecting an afternoon's diversion. Continue the entertainment." He ignored Middlebury, now looking rather foolish on the edge of the stage.

Ben expected a protest, but the deputy peered at the earl's company, smiled faintly, gracefully, and retired to a post nearby. Parkes hurried off after Middlebury and the other constable followed as well.

"The first scene is over, Master Ben Jonson. The second is about to begin," Shakespeare whispered as he passed into the tiring house. "Keep your eyes open and expect the unexpected. We shall trap the villains at their own game."

Before Ben could question him further, Shakespeare was gone. The prologue began at last. The play was on.

Eleven

bout your years, my lord," Ben moved about the stage, circling Burbage. They were in the first half of the play and Ben, dressed as a girl masquerading as a boy, was revealing his character's love for the Duke Orsino, Burbage's role.

"That's too old, by heaven," Burbage replied, shaking his head gravely. "Let still the woman take one older than herself; so wears she to him, so sways she level in her husband's heart. For, boy, however we do praise ourselves, our fancies are more giddy and unfirm, more longing, wavering, sooner lost and worn, than women's are."

"I think it well, my lord," Ben agreed. His acting had so consumed him that he hadn't had the chance to keep his eyes open as Shakespeare had instructed. But, even at that, nothing was out of the ordinary. The audience laughed when they were supposed to laugh. Players made their entrances and exits. All seemed well. Still, Ben thought as Burbage answered him, something was not right.

"Then let thy love be younger than thyself, or thy affection cannot hold the bent; for women are as roses, whose fair flow'r being once displayed, doth fall that very hour."

Ben sighed. "And so they are. Alas, that they are so, to die, even when they to perfection grow!"

And the play went on.

❧ ❧ ❧ ❧

"You are doing a fine job, Ben." Shakespeare patted his shoulder in the wings.

Ben mopped the sweat from his face. On stage, John Lambert, Arthur Digges, Peter Carew and another actor held sway, plotting the downfall of Malvolio, the villain of the play.

"Here comes my noble gull-catcher," an actor was saying.

"Wilt thou set a foot on my neck," answered Arthur Digges, looking comical with the padding in his stomach.

Ben turned away from the action and back to Shakespeare. "Half this sweat comes from worry, Master. Not from the labors of acting. What are we waiting for? What will happen?"

"Perhaps something, perhaps nothing. Time will tell."

"And if nothing happens?"

"Then, I suspect, we shall be arrested when the play ends. And Henry Condell will be sharing his cell with us. Tis a fine and private place, a dungeon. We shall keep each other's spirits up." Shakespeare winked at Ben.

"This is no laughing matter, Master."

"I'm not laughing."

"Come, Mistress Viola. Time for our entrance." Robert Armin appeared at Ben's elbow; he glared at Susanna Mayo. "Why is the girl back here, Will? Haven't we enough problems?"

"Concentrate on your part, Robert. You skipped a line in the last scene." The words were spoken gently, but Armin grunted and gripped Ben's arm tightly in reply.

Ben looked at Shakespeare as he and Armin stepped into the audience's view. His master winked again and Ben turned his attention back to the play. "Save thee, friend, and thy music. Dost thou live by thy tabor?"

"No, sir," Armin responded, dressed in his clown costume. "I live by the church."

"Art thou a churchman?"

And the play continued.

❧ ❧ ❧ ❧

Ben still wasn't sure what Shakespeare had in mind. Everything was as it should be. Well, he admitted to himself, some of the performances *were* a bit choppy. His own, for one. Lambert stumbled over his lines as Sir Andrew like he'd never seen them before. Were it not for Cuthbert Burbage feeding him like a baby, he would have been lost. Carew and Digges had their speeches down fine; it was the movements about the stage which spoiled their performances. Yet, nothing else was out of the ordinary.

The actor playing Fabian moved next to Ben. It was time for Fabian and Ben to re-enter. Ben sucked in his breath as they stepped out; the last performance of *Twelfth Night* had never gotten beyond this scene.

"He is as horribly conceited of him; and pants and looks pale, as if a bear were at his heels." Fabian walked beside Ben but addressed his lines to the overstuffed Arthur Digges standing near centerstage. At this point in the plot, a duel was being staged between Ben's character and Lambert's Sir Andrew Aguecheek.

Digges sidestepped as they drew near and looked to Ben. "There's no remedy, sir; he will fight with you for his oath's sake. Marry, he hath better bethought him of his quarrel, and he finds that now scarce to be worth talking of. Therefore draw, for the supportance of his vow. He protests he will not hurt you."

Ben was silent. John Lambert stood there in the costume of Sir Andrew Aguecheek. He studied Lambert for a long second.

It was not the same.

He was not the same.

Ben realized then that John Lambert did not kill Allan Hawkins. He was not the impostor.

"Ben!" Cuthbert Burbage hissed.

"Pray God defend me!" Ben snapped out of his trance and turned his face away from the other actors. "A little thing," he continued, "would make me tell them how much I lack of a man."

The revelation should have relaxed him, but Ben was unsettled by another thought. If Lambert were not the murderer, who was? He faced the others. The critical moment was about to arrive. Whatever Shakespeare had expected must happen soon.

"Give ground," Fabian counseled Ben, "if you see him furious."

Across the stage, Digges, as Sir Toby Belch, was consulting with John Lambert. "Come, Sir Andrew, there's no remedy. The gentleman will, for his honor's sake, have one bout with you. He cannot by the duello avoid it. But he has promis'd me, as he is a gentleman and a soldier, he will not hurt you. Come on; to it."

The actors gathered towards centerstage. From the corner of his eye, Ben saw Shakespeare watching, standing just in the shadows. His heart skipped a beat. The slim figure of Susanna Mayo stood next to the playwright.

Facing John Lambert, Ben held his breath and put his hand on the hilt of the sword dangling at his side.

"Pray God he keep his oath!" Lambert exclaimed, almost as much to the audience as to the other players.

A weak smile lit Ben's face as his next line came back to him. It was most suitable, for more than one reason. "I do assure you, tis against my will."

With that they drew their swords and eyed each other.

And nothing happened.

Just as it was supposed to be.

Ben exhaled and another actor, William Sly, made the entrance he had been denied in the last performance.

"Put up your sword," Sly ordered, playing the role of Antonio. "If this young gentleman have done offense, I take the fault on me; If you offend me, I for him defy you."

The point of Ben's sword drooped to the floor and Ben leaned on it as his shoulders sagged. The moment had passed.

Digges approached Sly with a sharp look in his eye.

"You, sir? Why, what are you?"

Ben scarcely heard Sly's reply. He was watching Digges. The preposterously padded Sir Toby was talking to William Sly even as he moved past him, and that was not in the play.

"Nay," Digges said. "If you be an undertaker, I am for you."

Both men drew their swords, but as Ben watched, Sir Toby Belch dove for Sir Andrew Aguecheek, not William Sly.

"Ben!"

The cry came from Shakespeare and Susanna.

Then, the look in Arthur Digges's eyes became clear. Ben flicked the point of his sword up and sped forward without thinking.

Digges's blade was aimed for John Lambert's unprotected stomach.

The needle-sharp point of the blade touched, pushed, and cut the fabric of Lambert's coat.

Lambert froze, his face ashen, unable to move.

Just as the shock on Lambert's face turned to pain, metal against metal sounded and Digges's sword was turned, clipping Lambert's cheek and starting a trickle of blood down his face.

Digges staggered back under Ben's parry. Eyes wide in surprise, he studied Ben for an instant. And then a crooked grin tilted his face. He slashed viciously, the blade whirring through the air.

Ben met steel with steel, and the clang echoed off the galleries. He staggered back, regained his balance, and thrust back with his own blade.

Digges, eyes blazing with fury, swept low, blocking Ben's thrust. He paused, taking Ben's measure, then he feinted quickly left and went right, trying to draw Ben off balance.

It worked.

Ben shifted to meet the threat and lost his footing. He tumbled to the floor. His foe stood above him, leering.

Staring up at his approaching death, Ben thought he saw gleaming metal blades encircle Digges's head. He didn't understand for a minute. Digges disappeared and a hand grabbed Ben by the arm and pulled him up. Shaking his head to clear it, Ben saw that the other players had finally acted, their sword points holding Digges motionless.

"Arthur Digges?" Ben asked Shakespeare, who had just pulled him to his feet.

The genial playwright nodded. "Arthur Digges."

"Arrest them!"

Geoffrey Middlebury stood, redfaced and puffing for breath, at the edge of the stage. "They should all be arrested! Tis but another example of the perversions of players."

The Earl of Southampton cocked his head to one side and smiled. "From this seat it looked as if the young man averted a tragedy. I see no reason to arrest anyone, but the scoundrel who just tried to stick his fellow there. And," he turned a withering look on Middlebury, "what right have you to order anyone's arrest here. You are out of your jurisdiction. No one will be arrested."

Middlebury's face grew more crimson and he stomped his foot. "But Constable Parkes is well within his rights." Middlebury hooked the quivering red-head's arm with his hand and dragged him forward. "Your Lordship, you must not allow them to get away free!"

"Hold!"

Ben couldn't remember ever hearing his master's voice raised that high.

"Master Middlebury has plenty of reason to want me arrested. To hide his own guilt for one. Don't let him leave!"

The other constable looked from the Earl to Shakespeare and back to the Earl again, then to Middlebury, and then to the Earl. Southampton nodded. The lawman moved behind the Deputy and waited patiently, hefting his club in his hand.

Parkes looked from Shakespeare to Middlebury, his heavy jowls shaking so hard that Ben thought his freckles might fall off, and shrugged. "I am at your service your Lordship." Parkes's voice quaked as he turned towards Southampton.

"What madness is this?" Middlebury ignored Parkes and puffed his chest out, his hair bristling like a rooster's comb.

"Check the boy's pocket." Shakespeare pointed to the vest stretched over Arthur Digges's padded stomach. "You'll find a note there ordering the boy to kill his fellow, a note Deputy Middlebury penned."

The other constable slipped his fingers into a small pocket and produced a crumpled bit of paper. He looked at it, and shrugged. He couldn't read.

John Donne stepped forward and took the piece of paper. "Master Shakespeare's right. It says, 'Kill Lambert.'"

"How did you know?" Ben asked.

"Never mind." His master's eyes were locked on Southampton. The Earl smiled at the playwright and turned to Clarence Parkes. "Arrest him." He pointed to the Deputy Sheriff.

"Your Lordship!" Parkes protested.

"Arrest him!"

Ben could almost see the anger infesting Middlebury's blood. For just a moment, Ben thought that Middlebury was going to attack Southampton, but the Deputy wasn't a wholly ignorant man and he spun—Parkes and the other constable joining him on either side—and tromped from the room.

The black-haired earl smiled across the bedlam erupting in the Globe and winked at Ben and Shakespeare.

❧ ❧ ❧ ❧

It took several minutes to straighten out the mess onstage. Richard Burbage looked more confused than ever. Cuthbert, ever the manager, was already preparing their properties for the next performance. The guards hauled a cursing Arthur Digges and a blustering Geoffrey Middlebury off to the Tower as a frightened Peter Carew tried to make his exit in all the confusion.

The extended foot of Susanna Mayo cut short Carew's escape. Round and trembling, Carew lay on the floor, mesmerized by Shakespeare's eyes.

"Please, Master. Don't hit me!"

Ben half-expected his master to hit Carew anyway, but then Shakespeare did an odd thing. He reached down and took Carew's hand in his. With more than just a little grunt, he pulled the boy to his feet.

"No one will hit you anymore, Master Carew. You have some

things to answer for, but I think I know the truth of it."

"Thank you, Master. Thank you!" Carew scampered back into a corner, staying out of everyone's way.

"Come, Ben. We've things to do."

A bloodied John Lambert was being bandaged in their path. He turned a pale face towards them and managed a weak grin. "I suppose I should thank you, Ben."

"Twouldn't be in character for you. The smile is enough."

"Middlebury said he had great plans for me," Lambert explained, his head drooping.

"Deadly plans, my boy," Shakespeare corrected. "Deadly plans."

Ben patted his one-time rival on the arm and followed Shakespeare across the floor and out of the Globe.

Standing in front of the theater, the elm trees waving in the evening breeze, Ben grabbed Shakespeare by the blouse and held him back. "But, Master. I don't understand. What did Allan Hawkins have to do with the Earl of Essex and Middlebury and Arthur Digges, and Peter Carew, and. . . ."

"Hush, lad. That tale's for another day," and Shakespeare smiled mysteriously.

Twelve

xplain this labyrinth, Will," Big Ben Jonson demanded, banging his tankard down for some quiet.

They were at the Mermaid Tavern on Bread Street. It was one of the red-headed giant's favorite haunts, and on this day he hosted a special group of friends.

John Donne was there. Harrison, of Stratford, was in attendance. And, of course, Shakespeare and his former apprentice, Ben Jonson, were the guests of honor. Even Susanna Mayo perched on a bench, though the barkeep's wife kept a close eye on her from the kitchen.

"What would you have me say?" Shakespeare asked.

"Let's start with the 'why'."

"To blacken the theaters, our theater in particular, at the outset," Shakespeare began. "Susanna held the key to the genesis of this tragedy. Allan Hawkins's uncle, who had married Allan's mother, was without money. He had practically bankrupted the shipping company his brother had built. This much, Susanna told us. Then, some Puritans, led by our friend Middlebury, offered to buy Hawkins out of his debts if he could convince Allan to wound one of his fellows onstage during a performance."

"Treachery most bold," Donne said.

"Aye," Shakespeare agreed. "The Puritans often nip at our heels, and they hate us with a passion. But to plot such a deceit, and be found out for it, would not win many friends for the Puritans. Allan wouldn't yield to their demands, and in a last effort to force him to the task, Hawkins sent his chief rogue to threaten Allan further."

"Simon Fry," Ben offered.

"Yes, Simon Fry," Shakespeare repeated. "The night before the murder, at the tavern, Fry told Allan that Susanna would be hurt if Allan didn't go along with their plan, and he must have let slip how deep the conspiracy went. Aye, Fry might have even mentioned Middlebury's connection to the Essex faction. Middlebury's objections to the theater have more to do with the Essex affair than his devout religious beliefs.

"Then, Master Middlebury learned, from Walter Hawkins probably, that Allan intended to run away, and he decided that Allan had to die. That would accomplish two objectives. One, they would eliminate someone who knew of their conspiracy. Second, the death of Allan onstage would serve their purpose far better than a mere wound. Ben was absolutely right in his analysis. Excesses of the theater! A murder committed on stage for the audience's pleasure. What better perversion could be perpetrated? Not to mention the fact that James of Scotland is a patron of the theater and such an episode would tarnish his chances of obtaining the English crown, at least for a little while. And the Puritans, as well as Middlebury, are anxious for him to be out of the running.

"Walter Hawkins was in a difficult position," Shakespeare continued. "Middlebury probably threatened to cut off his money if he didn't agree to the murder. So, Hawkins sent his rogue, Simon Fry, to help."

"A man kill his own blood? Seems unlikely," Harrison grumbled.

"His blood, but not his blood," Shakespeare pointed out. "He'd had no problem using Simon Fry to intimidate the lad; murder is only a half step further."

"That's why Hawkins acted strangely and didn't immediately ask about the body," Ben said slowly, finally understanding.

"Our questions worried him. Obviously, we didn't visit him just to deliver the news of Allan's death. Hawkins must have sent that man following us, the man that you encountered later, Ben."

"You've answered the 'why', Will, now show us the 'how'," the older Ben Jonson asked. "How was the murder on stage accomplished? Who is Arthur Digges? And how did you know that he was the murderer?"

"Arthur Digges, I suspect," Shakespeare answered, "was the pickpocket that Parkes arrested a month ago. . . ."

"Quick with his hands, he was," exclaimed Harrison eagerly.

"Just so," Shakespeare nodded. "And he was most assuredly Geoffrey Middlebury's watchdog. Middlebury didn't trust Allan Hawkins, so he arranged through his contacts in the merchants' community for Arthur to be released from jail, cleaned up, and apprenticed to the company to keep an eye on Allan. After the conspirators discovered that Allan planned to flee, Middlebury sent word to Digges to kill Allan. They managed to smuggle Simon Fry backstage to help. Henry was eliminated while Digges, who probably learned many of the lines as he picked pockets before his arrest, put the handkerchief to his face and killed Allan."

"But Peter Carew was with him!" Ben protested.

"He lied." Shakespeare was blunt. "When Mistress Mayo let us know that Allan didn't put the bruise on Peter's face, well, Carew had obviously lied. If he had lied about that, everything he had said was subject to question. He was bruised. Someone had done it. Who was Peter's constant companion?"

"Arthur Digges," Ben reluctantly replied.

"It all made perfect sense," Shakespeare continued. "When we got too close to Simon Fry, Digges killed him, showing his inexperience by leaving his dagger behind—the same dagger which had pinned the warning note to the wall in the tiring house, Ben."

"That's why Arthur had to borrow mine yesterday. He didn't have his; I'd thrown it in the Thames." Ben nodded in understanding.

"But what put you onto all this? What drew it all together?" Donne leaned forward, fascinated with the tale.

"Two nights ago at Ben Jonson's house, I knew that Middlebury was up to his eyeballs, but I wasn't sure how," Shakespeare continued. "Then, Susanna told me that Peter Carew had lied and Ben told me about his near brush with Digges while following the three apprentice boys, and of the later attack on Ben and the girl. Ben thought it was Lambert who had sent the rogues, but when did he have time? Hardly five minutes passed between their leaving Lambert and being attacked. Lambert couldn't have found three such scoundrels that quickly, but Digges had plenty of time. And, he knew where to find you."

Ben shook his head slowly, letting it all sink in. "So all that Lambert and Armin discussed had nothing to do with the murders."

"But everything to do with Robert's latest play." A gentle smile lit Shakespeare's face. "Lambert is such a toady that he played up to Robert. And Robert, needing praise as we all do, listened to everything Lambert said."

"Aye, I'll buy all that you have said," Big Ben Jonson began. "But how did you know that they would try something at the last performance?"

"A gamble, my friend. What better place to condemn the players to their final rest than at a command performance with a load of courtiers present. A second such murder, on the heels of the first, would seal our fate. I had to take the chance. I knew of no other way to force their hand."

"I don't argue with success, Will. But common sense wears a different coat," Harrison exclaimed. "Why would Digges do it? Committing a murder openly before an audience with no attempt to hide his face would assure that he would taste the executioner's axe.

"Why should he be concerned about the executioner? Wasn't his patron the Deputy High Sheriff of London?" Shakespeare reminded them. "Most likely he would have been allowed to escape. And then, some night, he'd end up floating in the Thames. He knows far too much. But now, seems the executioner will have double duty."

"What of Walter Hawkins?" John Donne asked.

"Nothing links Walter Hawkins with Allan's death, other than speculation. But, methinks he does not slide away unpunished."

"And how's that?" Ben queried.

"His shipping business will collapse without the Puritans paying his debts, and they have little reason to now. And his wife, I suspect, will be sorry that she told her husband of Allan's plan to run away with Susanna, for only she knew of that plan. Twill be a sad life he'll lead from now on," Shakespeare finished.

"Then, that's it," Harrison said, his sandy mustache drooping. "You've brought the affair to a close."

The others nodded in agreement.

"Not quite." Shakespeare's perpetual smile slipped into a frown, and he began slowly stroking his earring.

His audience turned towards the playwright in surprise.

"What do you mean, Will?" Big Ben Jonson leaned across the table.

"Yes, speak up, Will?" Harrison insisted.

"There's yet another conspirator in this affair. One unshackled by the law."

"Who, Master?" Young Ben Jonson was as thoroughly confused as his big namesake.

"Yes, and how? You've tied up all the loose ends," Donne protested.

"Almost, but some still dangle in the wind. Think of the timing backstage just before poor Allan was run through. Henry was already waiting to go onstage. Digges had not the time to help Fry carry Henry below and truss him up. Yet Henry remembered four hands holding him."

"So, there was a third person backstage." Ben nodded in understanding.

"But who?" Big Ben Jonson asked.

"One who belonged there. One who had the time to find his way around."

"Who, blast you!" Harrison exploded.

"You!" Shakespeare charged, pointing a slender finger at his childhood friend, no hint of a smile about his face.

Ben's mind was churning in confusion, but something in Harrison's ruddy complexion sent a quiver down his spine.

"You're daft, man." The carpenter showed little conviction in his rebuttal. He fidgeted in his seat.

"Am I?" Shakespeare stood and circled the table. "You had just been hired. From the shipyards, you told me. I'll wager that you worked for Walter Hawkins there."

"So what if I did. Proves nothing. What would profit me to be involved." A stubbornness masked Harrison's face.

"Money, and conviction. You told me how tough times were in Stratford. And I've known for years of your Puritan sentiments. Convenient that you came over to work the morning of the murder. Middlebury must have realized that he needed another pair of hands at the Globe."

A fine trickle of sweat reached down from Harrison's temple, dampening his mustache and he bit his lip. "But I was nowhere near the tiring house. I was out back, working on props."

"Aye," Shakespeare nodded grimly. "So you said. But Robert Armin, who has no reason to lie, saw you backstage just before Henry was assaulted. Watch him, Ben!"

The carpenter leapt up from the table, bowling it over in his haste. He dove towards the door, but Ben snagged his boot and sent him sprawling to the floor as his big namesake landed on Harrison's back.

Two constables raced in from the street and hauled the sputtering, cursing carpenter away. A quiet Shakespeare watched from the door as his boyhood friend was carried off.

"You have a flair for the dramatic, Master Shakespeare," a flustered Susanna Mayo announced moments later, straightening her dress as the table was put back in order.

Ben watched as his master turned his gentlest smile on the girl. "Twas necessary to make him run. He showed his guilt most clearly that way. And," Shakespeare paused for a fraction of a second, "I half-hoped he could prove his innocence. But twas not to be."

"Too many surprises. But, Will, one last question." Redheaded Ben Jonson grasped his tankard firmly and leaned across the table. "How were you able to arrange for the Queen to command a performance on such short notice? Companies would give their lives to appear once, yet you snap your fingers and magically an invitation appears."

Shakespeare tipped his own tankard up and sipped slowly. He winked at his friend and lightly fingered his earring. "Some things must remain secrets."

Big Ben Jonson frowned, started to speak, and then thought better of it.

Shakespeare turned to the lawyer. "You are a good man, John Donne. And played your part well. I would meet you again, and my friend Jonson here, to talk about more pleasant things—plays and poetry, perhaps."

"I was glad to be of service."

"And you, my young friend," the playwright turned to Ben. "I've found depths in you I never knew existed. You've grown to maturity before my very eyes and yet I saw it not. I'll not assign you lesser roles again. You were most necessary in bringing this matter to a close."

Ben squared his shoulders and smiled at his famous friend.

The group sat silent for a few moments. Nothing more seemed necessary. Ben couldn't erase the memory of Digges' anger at being thwarted. And now, that vision was matched by one of the sad-faced Harrison staring at his own executioner.

Saying their goodbyes, Jonson and Donne finally slipped out and away, leaving Shakespeare, Ben, and Susanna behind.

"Come, Ben Jonson, let us see Mistress Mayo home."

The trio left the Mermaid and headed towards the spire of St.

Paul's rising high above them. Ben found himself growing increasingly restless. Shakespeare was quiet, lost in his own thoughts it seemed.

Two blocks from the Mermaid, an ornate, gold-gilted carriage clattered down the street toward them. Ben paid little attention; his mind still buzzed at Harrison's treachery. And, he caught himself glancing sideways at Susanna Mayo, the memory of her hand in his as they raced through London lingering in his mind's eye. No other maiden had touched him like she had. No other had wrapped him in her eyes as tightly as she.

But the carriage drew up beside them and stopped with a fearful rattle. The door sprung open and a bearded man, brightly dressed in reds, silvers, and golds, hopped out.

"Master Shakespeare," he said, bowing low.

Ben watched as his master returned the greeting. The man with the fancy carriage seemed familiar. Ben had seen him before. With a snap of his fingers, Ben remembered. It was the Baron Rockford, who had come to see his master some days before. Susanna elbowed Ben, but he ignored her jab.

"Someone would like to see you," the Baron said to Shakespeare. Ben stepped back, but the Baron smiled at him. "You, too, young sir."

Ben steadied himself on the creaking frame and climbed into the coach, finding himself nose to nose with Queen Elizabeth.

"Ben Jonson. You are more handsome than that other brigand with your name. He is impertinent." Her voice was steady and confident, with a hint of a laugh in it. "But you are a young man of great courage. We are in your debt."

Ben knelt, staring up into the strong features of her face. He bowed his head and then felt a trembling hand laid on his shoulder.

"You bear watching," she continued. "Great things may be in store for you. Arise."

She withdrew her hand and Ben struggled to a seat as Shakespeare and Baron Rockford drew abreast of the door. They bowed and

Elizabeth motioned for them, too, to arise.

"Shakespeare. We have not had the pleasure of thanking you for your troubles in our behalf."

For the first time in his apprenticeship, Ben saw Shakespeare blush. "I did only what was necessary," the playwright murmured. "Would that the outcome had been less sorrowful for your Majesty."

"Kindness is a virtue you hold in plenty. The affair was painful; Essex was beloved."

"Essex?" Ben was scratching his head, the Queen forgotten. "Master, I'm confused."

"Young man, your Master has been in the Queen's service for some time. He played a key role in watching the Earl of Essex last year. Aye, key enough to almost catch Deputy Sheriff Middlebury with his pants down," Baron Rockford explained.

"But the inquisition. Master Burbage was questioned." Ben couldn't take it all in.

"A player may go many places and do many things," the Queen explained, "*if* no one suspects that he is doing other than being a player. Your master's service has been and must remain a secret.

"So you, too, young man, may come to be of service to us. Your Master sings your praises."

"He is a most remarkable man," Shakespeare said.

"Thank you all," the Queen finished.

"No, your Majesty. We thank you for helping us to bring this present affair to a close." Shakespeare bowed once more.

"It was a small thing, done with pleasure."

Ben climbed out and he and Shakespeare stepped back while Rockford entered the coach. "I'll call on you soon," the Baron cried as the carriage started bouncing on down the street.

"You have been interesting companions," Susanna Mayo exclaimed. "Murderers, conspirators, and queens. Tis been a fascinating sojourn. But I think I need rest before another." She broke the silence as they drew abreast of a pretty, half-timbered house.

"Is this home?" Ben asked.

"Aye, the place we never made it to that day. Come see me some time, when you're not chasing down murderers and being granted audiences with the Queen. You'll be quite welcome, Ben Jonson."

Those eyes captivated him once more and he smiled in spite of himself. "I will."

A moment later, she had disappeared inside the house. Shakespeare and Ben were alone again.

"Ben," Shakespeare said. "Ben!"

He tore his eyes away from the house and looked at the red cheeks of William Shakespeare. "Yes."

"Time to be off. Two days hence we open *Richard III.* You have lines to learn. Wenching is an occupation for another day. I may not be your master, but I am your employer."

"There's always something else," Ben complained.

"Yes." Shakespeare's eyes twinkled. "There's always something else. Have I told you about my new play?"

"No, you've been quite secretive," Ben reminded him as they started back down the lane towards the Thames.

"Tis about a Moor and his love for a young lady, . . ."

The End

Historical Notes

Writing historical fiction often requires that the author twist certain events to fit his plot. I've tried to avoid moving people and places around as much as possible. When it has happened, I have done so because I needed those people in those places at that time.

The Essex Rebellion of 1601 was one of the darkest moments during Queen Elizabeth's reign. Not that she was ever, seriously, in danger of being deposed, but as she so simply says it, "Essex was beloved." His defection hurt her deeply. The Globe Company was involved in just the way I have described. Although, strictly speaking, it was Augustine Phillips who was called to testify by the inquisition, not Richard Burbage. I substituted Burbage to keep the list of characters manageable. Essex did seek sanctuary with a London official, and the official did slip out his backdoor, as Essex came in the front, to prevent being tied to the rebellion. It was not a Deputy Sheriff Middlebury, however, who did this.

The Puritans hated the theater and all actors. The broadside quoted by Shakespeare came from an actual Puritan document of 1597 lambasting theaters and actors. Samuel Jonson's denunciation is taken primarily from a 1579 condemnation of an audience's behavior at a theater. The Globe, the Rose, and the other theaters were constantly in danger of being closed by the Puritan authorities. And it was the Puritan domination of London which drove the theaters outside the city limits. The zeal with which they pursued all manner of vice (as they defined it) knew few bounds.

As for young Ben Jonson, there is no record of William Shakespeare ever having an apprentice, but others of the Globe company certainly did. Apprentices were taken in by one of the adult actors, housed, fed, and trained. It is speculated that Shakespeare's younger brother, Edmund, was apprenticed to the King's Men before his unexplained death in 1607. Apprentices fulfilled much the role that I've assigned to them, though Richard

Burbage probably continued to play Romeo well past a convincing age before allowing a younger actor to step in. Upon completion of their apprenticeship, the young actors either joined the company, as Ben did, or they were attached to or moved on to another.

A word on dialogue and punctuation. To try to duplicate Elizabethan speech in a mystery novel would be to impose too heavy a burden on the reader. I've contemporized some of the vocabulary while trying to retain the flavor and beauty of the Elizabethan world. To have done otherwise would have slowed the action immeasurably. And, I have knowingly, and wittingly, eliminated the apostrophe before 'tis, 'twas, and 'twould to save the reader the irritation of having to see the pesky little creature so much.

Did Shakespeare, Ben Jonson, and John Donne know each other? Jonson and Shakespeare were known to have been friends. All three were certainly in London at the same time. Tradition tells us that the trio often met at the Mermaid Tavern on Bread Street, but documentary evidence of such gatherings is lacking. So the chance of an encounter moves from the realm of the unlikely to the possible.

Other fancies of mine: Big Ben Jonson and Shakespeare imply that *The Taming of the Shrew* was written about Jonson and his wife. In my defense, I can only tell you that the couple was married the same year that Shakespeare's play was first performed, and I must point out that Jonson himself referred to his wife, Anne, as a "shrew." Actual, painted, sets came after Elizabethan theater, but I have speculated that they might have been experimented with earlier. Shakespeare as Shylock? Scholars have said numerous times that this may have been a role which the Bard played. The famous Chandos portrait of Shakespeare is said to show the author in costume as Shylock (and is said to have been painted by none other than Richard Burbage himself). Finally, Shakespeare as secret agent for Queen Elizabeth? No defense; but isn't it fun to think about. I *will* point out that Shakespeare's contemporary, Christopher Marlowe, was almost certainly an agent.

Other errors, and there are always some, I take full responsibility for. The readers of my early drafts did a fine job in pointing out and helping me correct errors.

About the Author

Photo - Richard Gross

Tony Hays is a native of Madison and Murfreesboro, Tennessee. Holding degrees in History, Educational Psychology, and English, Hays has published extensively in the field of local history, and his short fiction has appeared in over ten different publications. He has raised goats, worked at a sawmill, been a veterinarian's assistant, served as foster-father to orphan cats, managed university residence halls, worked as a freelance writer, and taught English in Japan. A member of Mystery Writers of America, he teaches English at Motlow State Community College in Tullahoma, Tennessee and is married to his illustrator, Holly Lentz-Hays. Striper and Cleopatra Cat graciously share their home in Manchester with Holly and Tony.